"I would ha

"I thought about it," he said. "But you've done enough helping with the babies."

"I thought perhaps that you and I were about more than the babies, but maybe I was wrong," she said, looking away.

His heart slamming against his rib cage, he cupped her chin and swiveled it toward him. "You were right. You know you were."

Her eyes darkened with emotion and she stepped closer. She moved against him and slid her arms upward around his neck. She pulled his face toward hers and he couldn't remember feeling this alive. Ever.

His body was on full tilt in the arousal zone. He took a quick breath and forced himself to draw back. "I'm not sure I can pull back after this," he said. "If you're going to say no, do it now."

"Yes," she whispered. "Yes."

Dear Reader,

Have you ever been underestimated? How did you deal with it? Laugh it off? Get angry and stomp your foot? Ignore it?

All are options. For Princess Bridget Devereaux, once her life was saved by her now sister-in-law, everything changed. Now, she needs to make sure the life she's living is worth saving. What a challenge. What she doesn't know is that she is far more important than she believed.

So back to this underestimation thing.… Have you ever underestimated yourself? I think we often do. When someone comes along who believes in you, who sees you as bigger and more capable than you see yourself, it can be a hugely empowering, amazing experience.

When Princess Bridget meets Dr. Ryder McCall, he and his babies challenge her in ways she'd never dreamed. Along the way, they could end up saving each other. I hope you'll enjoy the ride to see how it all turns out.…

xo,

Leanne Banks

THE DOCTOR TAKES A PRINCESS

LEANNE BANKS

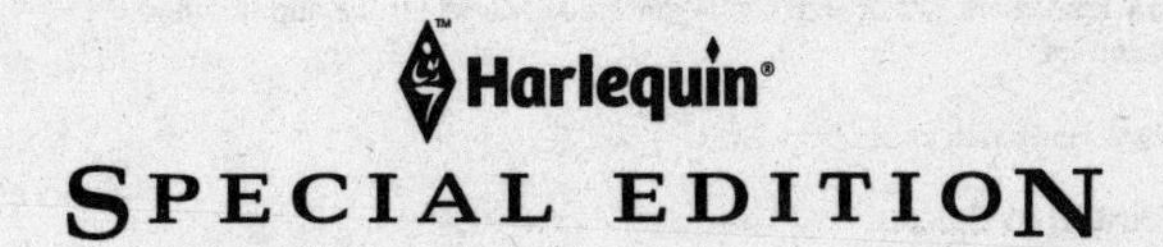

Recycling programs for this product may not exist in your area.

ISBN-13: 978-0-373-65609-7

THE DOCTOR TAKES A PRINCESS

This edition published by arrangement with Harlequin Books S.A.

For questions and comments about the quality of this book please contact us at Customer_eCare@Harlequin.ca.

www.Harlequin.com

Printed in U.S.A.

Books by Leanne Banks

Silhouette Special Edition

Royal Holiday Baby #2075
The Prince's Texas Bride #2115

Harlequin Special Edition

The Doctor Takes a Princess #2127

Silhouette Desire

**Royal Dad* #1400
Tall, Dark & Royal #1412
**His Majesty, M.D.* #1435
The Playboy & Plain Jane #1483
**Princess in His Bed* #1515
Between Duty and Desire #1599
Shocking the Senator #1621
Billionaire's Proposition #1699
†Bedded by the Billionaire #1863
†Billionaire's Marriage Bargain #1886
Blackmailed Into a Fake Engagement #1916
†Billionaire Extraordinaire #1939
From Playboy to Papa! #1987
***The Playboy's Proposition* #1995
***Secrets of the Playboy's Bride* #2002
CEO's Expectant Secretary #2018

*The Royal Dumonts
†The Billionaires Club
**The Medici Men

LEANNE BANKS

is a *New York Times* and *USA TODAY* bestselling author who is surprised every time she realizes how many books she has written. Leanne loves chocolate, the beach and new adventures. To name a few, Leanne has ridden on an elephant, stood on an ostrich egg (no, it didn't break), gone parasailing and indoor skydiving. Leanne loves writing romance because she believes in the power and magic of love. She lives in Virginia with her family and four-and-a-half-pound Pomeranian named Bijou. Visit her website at www.leannebanks.com.

This book is dedicated to all those
underestimated women with tender hearts and
big fears who hide it all with a big smile. Thank you
for being so much more than we give you credit for.

Prologue

Ryder McCall raced the double baby stroller into the elevator just as the doors started to close. The twin boys cackled with glee at the wild ride as he pressed the button for the eighth floor. He'd already rescheduled the appointment with his attorney three times and he would have done it again if he'd known the nanny was going to bail on him. Again.

In the back of his mind, he counted his pulse. His heart rate was higher now than when he'd run a half marathon last year. His life was far different now, he thought as he glanced at the boys and caught a swishing movement behind him. Stepping to the side, he saw a woman dressed in a pink cocktail gown that skimmed over her creamy shoulders and her curvy body. The dress ended just above her knees, revealing a tempting glimpse of her legs and high-heeled sandals. The medical expert in him knew the negative impact of high heels on the human body, but the man in him was trying to remember the last time he'd been out with a woman. He was having a tough time remembering.

The woman smiled at him and gestured toward the twins. "They're adorable. I bet they keep you busy."

He nodded. "More than you could—"

The elevator suddenly jolted and dropped several feet, then stopped.

Ryder glanced at the boys at the same time he heard the woman's intake of breath. "Everyone okay?"

The twins just looked at them with wide eyes.

"Are we stuck?" the woman asked, her brow furrowed with worry.

"Let me see," he said and pushed the button for another floor. The elevator didn't move. He pushed the button to open the doors and nothing happened. He pushed the alarm button and a piercing sound filled the elevator.

The woman covered her ears. "Oh, my—"

A voice came on an intercom. "This is building security. Do you have a problem?"

"We're stuck," Ryder yelled over the terrible pulsating alarm. He heard a sob from one of the boys. A half beat later, the other started, louder.

"So sorry, sir. We'll come and fix it soon."

"Soon," he echoed as the twins began to cry in earnest. "When is soon?"

"As soon as possible," the woman on the intercom said and there was a clicking noise. The alarm shut off, but the boys were in high gear.

"Oh, the poor things. They must be frightened," the woman in the elevator said. She paused a moment, then shrugged. "Here, I'll hold one of them."

Ryder shot a skeptical glance at her. "They haven't had their baths and they're very messy eaters." Tyler was wearing a gross combination of yellow and orange on his blue shirt while Travis clearly had not enjoyed his strained peas. Green smudges decorated the light blue shirt that matched his brother's.

The woman made a tsking sound. "Well, we have to do something. We can't let them keep screaming." She set her purse on the floor and held out her hands. "Go ahead, give one of them to me," she insisted in a voice that sounded as if she were accustomed to having her orders followed.

As a medical doctor and acting chief adviser for the residents at Texas Medical Center, he, too, was accustomed to having his orders followed. This time, though, he decided to allow the woman to take Tyler because the baby was clearly beyond upset. As soon as he set the boy in her arms, she bobbed as if she'd handled a crying baby before. Ryder hauled Travis out of his stroller seat and also bobbed.

The woman made soothing sounds and Tyler gradually quieted between hiccups. As usual, Travis took a little longer. He was the louder boy of the two.

"That's better," she said. "Who am I holding?"

"Tyler," Ryder said. "This is Travis. I'm Ryder McCall. Thank you for your help."

"You're quite welcome," she said in a voice that seemed to combine several accents, none of which originated from Texas. "I'm Bridget," she said and fanned herself with the shawl draped over her arm. "Whew, it's getting warm already."

"And it's only going to get hotter until they fix the elevator. Are you feeling faint?" he asked, aware that plenty of people would grow light-headed in this situation.

She shook her head. "No."

"I'd offer you some water, but I was in a hurry when I left the house, so all I've got are bottles for the boys."

"Well, at least you have that," she said and glanced at her watch. "I hope we're not stuck for long. Perhaps I should call my friends." She bent toward the floor and shook her head. "I'm sorry, Tyler. I'm going to have to put you down for a moment," she murmured and carefully placed the tot in his stroller seat. She picked up her phone and punched some numbers, then frowned.

"Let me guess," Ryder said. "No service."

She nodded.

"Figures. The steel doors can sustain most catastrophes known to man, so they're bound to make it difficult to get a cell connection."

She bit her lip and winced. "Oh, I wonder if someone will call my security."

"They're on their way," he said, wondering if she hadn't understood the conversation he'd had with the woman earlier. Maybe she hadn't heard correctly, he thought, between the alarm bleeping and the boys screaming. "At least, they better be on their way. I hope the boys don't—"

"Need a diaper change?" she asked, nodding in understanding. "Time for the—"

"Nanny," he said in complete agreement. "I just wish I could find one who would stay around longer than two weeks."

"That sounds difficult. Are you working with an agency?"

He nodded. "Part of the problem is I work long hours."

"Hmm, and your wife?"

"I don't have a wife," he said.

Her eyes widened. "Oh, that must make it very difficult."

Ryder sighed. "I'm actually the boys' godfather. My brother and his wife were killed in an automobile accident one month ago."

Bridget gasped. "That's terrible. Those poor boys, and you, oh my goodness. Do you have any help at all?"

"Not unless I hire them," he muttered. "Do you have any children?"

She shook her head quickly, the same way he would have before he'd learned he would be raising the boys. "Two baby nieces," she said.

"That's how you knew to bob up and down with Tyler," he said.

"Yes," Bridget said and glanced at her watch again, growing uneasy. She'd agreed to the charity appearance she would be attending as a favor to her sister's longtime friend, and her security was only a three-button code away if she should need them. If her sister's friend became uneasy, however, she might call Valentina.

Valentina might call security to check on her and… She shuddered at the public scene that would cause. Bridget was here in Dallas to do the job her brother had asked of her and as soon as she was done, she was off to Italy.

It was so warm that she was getting past the glow stage. Right now, she probably looked like she'd just finished a spinning class, although she did those as rarely as possible. Getting sweaty wouldn't matter that much to her if she weren't being photographed. During the last year and a half, however, it had been drilled into her that her appearance in front of the camera was a reflection of her country. It was her duty to look immaculate and to avoid scandal at all cost.

Bridget had slipped a few times on both counts. She might be a princess, but she wasn't perfect. Nor was she particularly patient. She could tell that Ryder, the other adult in the elevator, wasn't patient either. He was glancing upward as if he were assessing the structure of the lift.

"You're not thinking of climbing out, are you?" she couldn't resist asking.

"If no one shows up, I may have to," he said.

"And what were you planning to do with the babies?" she demanded, panicked at the prospect of being left alone with the twins. Now that she thought of it, Ryder's presence had made her feel much more reassured.

He shot her a level look. "The purpose of getting out would be to ensure safety for all of us."

He looked like a no-nonsense kind of man, strong, perhaps intolerant of anyone weaker than himself.

Which would include her. Okay, she was making assumptions. But what else could she bloody do? She was stuck in an elevator with the man. She couldn't deny the appeal of his strong jaw and lean but muscular body. She also couldn't deny her admiration that he had taken on his brother's orphaned twins.

An instant parent of twin boys? The mere thought made her sweat even more. Bridget would have forced herself to accept her responsibility in such a situation, but hopefully with sufficient support. Multiple children, multiple nannies.

She sighed, glancing at the emergency button. "We've heard nothing. Do you think we should call again?"

"It will make the boys cry again," he said, clearly torn.

"I'll take Tyler," she said and picked up the baby. He flashed her a smile that gave her a burst of pleasure despite their situation. "You're a little flirt, aren't you?" she said and tickled his chin.

Ryder stabbed the button and the shrieking alarm started. Tyler's smile immediately fell and his eyes filled with fear. He began to scream. His brother began to wail.

Seconds later, the alarm stopped and a voice came on the intercom, but Bridget couldn't make out the conversation with Ryder as she tried to comfort Tyler. The only thing she knew was that Ryder had spoken in a firm, commanding voice that rivaled that of her brother's, and anyone in their right mind had better obey.

The intercom voice went away, but the babies still cried. Bridget and Tyler bobbed. "What did they say?"

"They said they would take care of us in five minutes," he yelled over the cries of the boys.

"How did you do that?"

"I told them I was climbing out in three," he said.

"Effective. I wonder if I should try that sometime," she mused. "Is there anything else we can do to settle them down?" she asked loudly, still shielding Tyler's closest ear with her hand.

A long-suffering expression crossed his face. "Just one thing," he said. "Row, row, row your boat, gently down the stream."

Bridget stared in amazement at this man who reminded her of a modern-day warrior singing a children's song and something inside her shifted. The sensation made her feel light-headed. Alarm shot through her. Or perhaps, it was the heat. Pushing the odd feeling and any self-consciousness aside, she sang along.

Six minutes later, the elevator doors opened with a swarm of firemen, paramedics and Bridget's security guard standing outside.

"Your Highness," her security guard said, extending his hand to her.

"Just a second," she said, putting Tyler into his stroller seat.

"Your Highness?" Ryder echoed, studying her with a curious gaze. "Why didn't you—"

"It—it causes a fuss," she said. "Will you be okay? Will the children be okay?"

"We're fine," he said, and she felt foolish for questioning such a capable man.

"Well, thank you," she said and extended her hand

to his, noting that his hands were smooth, but large and strong. She felt an odd little spark and immediately pulled back. "And good luck."

"Your Highness, a medical professional is waiting to examine you," her security said as she stepped off the lift.

"I don't need a medical professional," she murmured. "I need a cosmetic miracle."

Chapter One

Sitting at the kitchen table of her brother-in-law's ranch, Bridget watched Zach Logan hug her sister Valentina as if he were leaving for a yearlong journey. Instead, she knew he would be gone for only a couple of nights. Bridget resisted the urge to roll her eyes. Zach and Valentina just seemed so gooey in love.

"Call me if you need anything," he told her, then swung his young daughter, Katiana, up into his arms. "Are you going to be good for your mommy?"

Katiana solemnly nodded.

"Give me a kiss," he said.

The toddler kissed his cheek and wrapped her little arms around his neck.

Despite her earlier reaction, the scene tugged at Bridget's heart. She knew Zach and Tina had gone through some tough times before they'd gotten married.

Zach shot Bridget a firm glance that instinctively

made her sit up straighter. He was that kind of man, confident with a strong will. Although she was happy Tina had found happiness with him, Bridget knew she would want a totally different kind of man. Charming, average intelligence, playful and most likely Italian.

"You," he said, pointing his finger at Bridget. "Stay out of elevators."

She laughed. "I can only promise that for a few days. When I go back to Dallas, I'm sure I'll have to face more elevators if I'm going to complete Stefan's latest job for me. If I have anything to do with it, I'm going to take care of it as quickly as possible."

Tina shot her a sideways glance. "Are you saying you're already tired of us?"

Bridget shook her head and walked to give her sister a hug. "Of course I'm not tired of you. But you know I've had a dream of having a long-delayed gap year in Italy and studying art for years now. I want to make that dream come true while I'm still young."

Tina made a scoffing sound, but still returned the hug. "You're far from losing your youth, but I agree you deserve a break. You've taken on the bulk of public appearances since I left Chantaine and moved here. I don't understand why you didn't take a break before coming here. I'm sure Stefan would have let you."

Stefan, their brother, the crown prince, could be the most demanding person on the planet, but what Tina said was true. He not only would have allowed Bridget a break, he had also encouraged it. "I want a year. A whole year. And he believes Chantaine needs more doctors. I agree. Especially after what happened to Eve—"

Her voice broke, taking her by surprise. She'd thought she'd gotten her feelings under control.

Tina patted her back with sympathy. "You still feel guilty about that. I know Eve wishes you didn't."

Bridget took a careful breath, reining in her emotions. "She saved my life when the crowd was going to stampede me. Pushed me aside and threw herself in front of me. I'm just so glad she survived it and recovered. I don't know what I would do if she hadn't…" Her throat closed up again.

"Well, she survived and you did, too. That's what's important," Zach said and pulled Bridget into a brotherly hug. "And now that you're in my territory, I want you to think twice before getting on elevators."

Tina laughed. "So protective," she said. "It's a wonder he doesn't find some kind of testing device for you to use so you won't get stuck again."

Zach rubbed his chin thoughtfully. "Not a bad idea. Maybe—"

"Forget it," Bridget said, the knot in her chest easing at the love she felt from both her sister and her brother-in-law. "I'll be fine. Think about it. How many people do you know who have gotten stuck in elevators? Especially more than once?"

"You were a good soldier," Tina said in approval. "And you still showed up for your appearance at Keely's charity event."

"She probably wasn't expecting me in my sad state with droopy hair and a dress with baby-food stain on it."

"Oh, she said they loved you. Found you charming.

Were delighted by your story about the elevator. Most important, the donations increased after your arrival."

"Well, I guess baby-food stains are good for something, then. I'll leave you two lovebirds to finish your goodbyes in private. Safe travels, Zach."

"You bet," he said.

Bridget scooped up her cup of hot tea and walked upstairs to the guest room where she was staying. Her sister had redecorated the room in soothing shades of green and blue. The ranch should have given Bridget a sense of serenity. After all, she was miles from Stefan and his to-do list for her. She was away from Chantaine where she was recognized and haunted by the paparazzi whenever she left the palace. But Bridget never seemed to be able to escape the restlessness inside her. That was why she'd decided to skip a short vacation and take care of this significant task Stefan had asked of her. After that, she could take her trip to Italy and find her peace again.

No one had ever accused Bridget of being deep. She voiced her distress and upset to her family at will, but presented the rest of the world with a cheery effervescent face. It was her job.

Some of the conditions she'd witnessed during the past year and a half, the sights and sounds of children sick in the hospital, Chantaine's citizens struggling with poverty, cut her to the quick and it had been difficult to keep her winsome attitude intact. It irritated her how much she now had to struggle to maintain a superficial air. Life had been so much easier when she hadn't faced others in need. Life had been easier when someone hadn't been willing to sacrifice her life for the sake of Bridget's safety.

Even though Eve had indeed survived and thrived since the accident, something inside Bridget had changed. And she wasn't sure she liked it. Eve and Stefan had fallen in love and married. Eve cared for Stefan's out-of-wedlock daughter as if she were her own. On the face of it, everything was wonderful.

Deep down, though, Bridget wondered if her life was really worth saving. What had she done that made her worthy of such an act?

She squeezed her eyes shut and swore under her breath. "Stop asking that question," she whispered harshly to herself.

Steeling herself against the ugly swarm of emotions, Bridget set her cup of tea on the table. She would complete the task Stefan asked of her. Then maybe she would have settled the score inside her, the score she couldn't quite explain even to herself. Afterward she would go to Italy and hopefully she would find the joy and lightness she'd lost.

After three days of being unable to meet with the head of residents at Texas Medical Center of Dallas, Bridget seethed with impatience. Dr. Gordon Walters was never available, and all her calls to his office went unanswered. Thank goodness for connections. Apparently Tina's friend Keely knew a doctor at University Hospital and there just happened to be a meet and greet for interns, doctors and important donors at a hotel near the hospital on Tuesday night.

Bridget checked into the hotel and her security took the room next to hers. One advantage of being at Zach's ranch meant security was superfluous. Not so in Dallas. She dressed carefully because she needed to impress and to be taken seriously. A black dress with heels. She resisted the urge to paint her lips red. The old Bridget wouldn't have batted an eye.

Frowning into the bathroom mirror in her suite, she wondered what that meant. Well, hell, if Madonna could wear red lipstick and be taken seriously, why couldn't she? She smoothed her fingers over her head and tucked one side of her hair behind her left ear. She'd colored her hair darker lately. It fit her mood.

She frowned again into the mirror. Maybe she would dye it blond when she moved to Italy.

She punched the code for her security on her cell phone. Raoul picked up immediately. "Yes, Your Highness."

"I'm ready. Please stay in the background," she said.

"Yes, ma'am. But I shall join you on the elevator."

A couple moments later, she rode said elevator to the floor which held the meeting rooms and ballrooms. A host stood outside the ballroom which housed the cocktail party she would attend. "Name?" he asked as she approached him.

She blinked, unaccustomed to being screened. Doors opened at the mention of her title. Not in Texas, she supposed. "Bridget Devereaux and escort," she said, because Raoul was beside her.

The man flipped through several pages and checked off her name. "Welcome," he said. "Please go in."

"The nerve of the man," Raoul said as they entered the ballroom full of people. "To question a member of the royal family," he fumed as he surveyed the room.

Bridget smiled. "Novel experience," she said. "I'm looking for Dr. Gordon Walters. If you see him, by all means, please do tell me."

Thirty minutes later, Bridget was ready to pull out her hair. Every time she mentioned Dr. Walters's name, people clammed up. She couldn't squeeze even a bit of information about the man from anyone.

Frustrated, she accepted a glass of wine and decided to take another tack.

Dr. Ryder McCall checked his watch for the hundredth time in ten minutes. How much longer did he need to stay? The latest nanny he'd hired had seemed okay when he'd left tonight, but after his previous experiences, he couldn't be sure. He caught a glimpse of the back of a woman with dark brown wavy hair and paused. Something about her looked familiar.

The dress was classic and on a woman with a different body, it would have evoked images of that actress. What was her name? Audrey something. But this woman had curves which evoked entirely different thoughts. The sight of the woman's round derriere reminded Ryder of the fact that he hadn't been with a woman in a while. Too long, he thought and adjusted his tie.

Curious, he moved so that he could catch a side view of her. Oh yeah, he thought, his gaze sliding over her feminine form from her calves to her thighs to the thrust of her breasts. He could easily imagine her minus the dress. His body responded. Then he glanced upward to her face and recognition slammed into him.

The woman speaking so animatedly to one of his

top residents, Timothy Bing, was the same woman he'd met in the elevator the other night. Princess whatever. Bridget, he recalled. And of course, his top resident was utterly enthralled. Why wouldn't he be? The poor resident was sleep-deprived, food-deprived and sex-deprived.

Ryder was suffering from the same deprivation albeit for different reasons. He wondered why she was here tonight. Might as well cure his curiosity, he thought, if he couldn't cure his other deprivations. He walked toward the two of them.

Timothy only had eyes for Her Highness. Ryder cleared his throat. Both Timothy and the woman turned to look at him.

Timothy stiffened as if he were a marine and he'd just glimpsed a superior. Ryder almost wondered if he would salute. "Dr. McCall," he said.

Bridget looked at him curiously. "Doctor?" she echoed. "I didn't know you were a doctor."

"We didn't have much time to discuss our occupations. Your Highness," he added.

Out of the corner of his vision, he saw Timothy's eyes bulge in surprise. "Highness," he said. "Are you a queen or something? I thought you said you were a representative of Chantaine."

Bridget shot Ryder a glare, then smiled sweetly at Timothy. "I am a representative of Chantaine. A royal representative, and I hope you'll consider the proposal I gave you about serving in Chantaine for a couple of years in exchange for a scholarship and all your living expenses."

Ryder stared at the woman in horrified silence. She

was trying to seduce away one of his prized residents. Timothy was brilliant. His next step should be to one of the top neurological hospitals in the States.

Ryder laughed. "Not in a million years," he said.

Bridget furrowed her brow. "Why not? It's a generous offer. Dr. Bing would benefit, as would Chantaine."

"Because Dr. Bing is not going to make a gigantic misstep in his career by taking off for an island retreat when he could be one of the top neurological surgeons in America."

Bridget's furrow turned to a frown. "I find it insulting that you consider a temporary move to Chantaine a misstep. Our citizens suffer from neurological illnesses, too. Is it not the goal of a doctor to heal? Why should there be a prejudice against us just because we reside in a beautiful place? Does that mean we shouldn't have treatment?"

"I wasn't suggesting that your country doesn't deserve medical care. It's my job, however, to advise Dr. Bing to make the best decisions in advancing his career and knowledge."

Princess Bridget crossed her arms over her chest and looked down her nose at him. "I thought that was Dr. Gordon Walters's job, although the man is nowhere to be found."

Timothy made a choking sound. "Excuse me," he said. "I need to…" He walked quickly away without finishing his sentence.

"Well, now you've done it," she said. "I was having a perfectly lovely conversation with Dr. Bing and you ruined it."

"Me?"

"Yes, you. The whole tenor of our conversation changed when you appeared. Dr. Bing was actually open to considering my offer to come to Chantaine."

"Dr. Bing wanted to get into your pants," Ryder said and immediately regretted his blunt statement.

Bridget shot him a shocked glance. "You're the most insulting man I've ever met."

"You clearly haven't met many residents," he said wearily. "I apologize if I offended you, but Timothy Bing doesn't belong in Chantley or wherever you said you're from."

"Chantaine," she said between gritted teeth. "I will accept your apology if you can direct me to Dr. Gordon Walters. He is the man I must meet."

Ryder sighed. "I'm afraid I'm going to have to disappoint you. Dr. Gordon Walters is not here tonight. He hasn't been working in the position as chief resident adviser for some time. It's not likely he'll return."

She cocked her head to one side and frowned further. "Then who will take his place?"

"No one will take his place. Dr. Walters is rightfully loved and respected. I am serving as his temporary successor."

Realization crossed her face. "How wonderful," she said, when she clearly found the news anything but.

Bloody hell, Bridget thought, clenching her fingers together. Now she'd put herself in a mess. She took a deep breath and tried to calm herself. Yes, she and Dr. McCall had engaged in a spirited discussion, but surely he would come around once he heard more about Chantaine and the program she was offering.

"Well, I'm glad I've finally found the person who is currently in charge. Our first meeting in the elevator showed that you and I are both responsible, reasonable adults. I'm sure we'll be able to come to an understanding on this matter," she said, imbuing her words with every bit of positive energy she could muster.

Dr. McCall shot her a skeptical glance. "I'll agree with your first point, but I can't promise anything on the second. It's good to see you again, Your Highness." His gaze gave her a quick sweep from head to toe and back again. "Nice dress. Good evening," he said and turned to leave.

It took Bridget an extra second to recover from the understated compliment that inexplicably flustered before she went after him. "Wait, please," she said.

Dr. McCall stopped and turned, looking at her with a raised eyebrow. "Yes?"

"I really do need to discuss Chantaine's medical needs with you. I'm hoping we can come to some sort of agreement."

"I already told you I couldn't recommend that Timothy Bing spend two years in your country," he said.

"But you have other students," she said. "I'm sure you have students interested in many different areas of medical care. Coming to Chantaine would enable the physicians to get hands-on experience. Plus there's the matter of the financial assistance we would offer."

"I'm sorry, Your High—"

"Oh, please," she said, unable to contain her impatience. "Call me Bridget. We've sung together in an elevator, for bloody sake."

His lips twitched slightly. "True. Bridget, I'm not

sure I can help you. Again, my number-one priority is guiding my students to make the best career decisions."

Her heart sank. "Well, the least you can do is give me an opportunity to discuss Chantaine's needs and what we have to offer."

He sighed and shrugged his shoulders in a discouraging way, then pulled a card from his pocket. "Okay. Here's my card. My schedule is very busy, but call my assistant and she'll work you in."

Work her in. Bridget clenched her teeth slightly at the words, but forced a smile. "Thank you. You won't regret it."

"Hmm," he said in a noncommittal tone and walked away.

She barely resisted the urge to stick out her tongue at him.

Raoul appeared by her side. "Are you all right, Your Highness? You look upset."

"I do?" she asked, composing herself into what she hoped look like a serene expression. She was finding it more and more difficult to pull off instant serenity these days. "I'm fine," she said. "I've just encountered a slight obstacle to completing my assignment for Chantaine."

She watched Ryder McCall's broad shoulders and tall form as he wove through the crowd. Slight obstacle was putting it mildly, but she'd learned that a positive attitude could get a woman through a lot of tricky spots. "I need to know everything about Dr. Ryder McCall by morning, if not before," she muttered and glanced around the room. It was amazing what one could learn about a person in a social situation such as this. She might as well make the best of it.

* * *

Ryder walked into his house braced for chaos. His home life had become one big state of chaos bigger than the state of Texas since he'd inherited his brother's boys. Instead of pandemonium, his home was dark and quiet, except for the sound of a baseball game. Ryder spotted his longtime pal Marshall lounging on the leather couch with a box of half-eaten pizza on the coffee table and a beer in his hand.

"Your sitter called me," Marshall said, not rising. "As your official backup. She said one of her kids got sick, so she couldn't stay. Just curious, where am I on that backup list?"

Pretty far down, Ryder thought, but didn't admit it. There were two middle-aged neighbors, an aunt on the other side of town and his admin assistant before Marshall. Ryder suspected he'd called in favors too often if everyone had refused but Marshall. "Thanks for coming. How are the boys?"

Marshall cracked a wily grin. "Great. Gave them a few Cheerios, wore them out and tossed them into bed."

"Bath?" he asked.

"The sitter took care of that before I got here. That Travis is a pistol. Didn't want to go to sleep, so I gave him my best Garth Brooks."

Ryder gave a tired smile. "Must have worked. I'll give a quick check and be right back."

"Cold one's waiting," Marshall said.

Ryder trusted Marshall to a degree, but he didn't think leaving the kids with his buddy from high school on a regular basis was a good idea. He wouldn't put it past Marshall to slip the boys a sip from his beer if he was desperate enough. When pressured, Marshall could get a little too creative, like the time he hot-wired the car of one of the school's top wrestlers because his own car had died.

Marshall owned a chain of auto-mechanic shops across Texas. He wore his hair in a ponytail and tattoos were stamped over his arms and back. He hadn't attended college, but he'd made a success of himself. Most people couldn't understand their friendship because they appeared to be total opposites, but a mutual appreciation for baseball, some shared holiday dinners which had always included hotdogs and hamburgers and the fact that they both tried to show up during the hard times had made them like family.

With his brother Cory gone, Marshall was the closest thing to family Ryder had. His gut twisted at the thought, but he shoved the feeling aside and gently opened the door to the nursery. He'd learned to walk with stealthlike quiet during the last month. The possibility of waking the boys made him break into a cold sweat.

Moving toward the closest crib, he glanced inside and even in the dark, he knew that this was Tyler, and he was in Travis's bed. Travis was in Tyler's bed. He wasn't going to complain. They were both lying on their backs in la-la land. Which was exactly where he would like to be.

Instead, he walked on quiet footsteps out of the room and gently closed the door behind him. Returning to the den, he saw Marshall still sprawled on his sofa with the same beer in his hand.

"They're asleep," Ryder said and sank into a leather chair next to the sofa. He raked his hand through his hair.

"I coulda told you that," Marshall said. "I made sure they would sleep well tonight."

He shot a quick glance at Marshall. "You didn't give them any booze, did you?"

Marshall looked offended. "Booze to babies? What kind of nut job do you think I am?"

"Well, you aren't around kids very much," Ryder said.

"Maybe not now, but I was an in-demand babysitter in junior high school. Some things you don't forget. And just in case you're worried, this is my second beer. I wouldn't go on a bender when I was taking care of your kids."

Chagrined, Ryder rubbed his chin. "You got me. Sorry, bud. Being in charge of two kids is making me a little crazy."

"A little?" Marshall said and shook his head. "You've turned into the nut job. You know what your problem is, you're no fun anymore. Those babies sense it and it gets them all uptight, too. It's like a virus. You spread it to the babysitters and it makes them crazy, so they quit. You need to get laid and go to a ball game."

"Thanks for the advice," Ryder said. "I'll take your advice in a decade or so."

"Lord help us if you wait that long," Marshall said. "Maybe I could set you up with somebody. Take the edge off."

Ryder slid him a sideways glance. "I'll pass. You and

I may root for the Texas Rangers, but we don't share the same taste in women."

"Your loss," Marshall said, sitting upright. "I know some women who could wear you out and make you sleep like a baby."

"I've learned babies don't always sleep that well."

"It's your aura," Marshall said. "That's what Jenny, my ex, would say. Your aura is poisoning your environment."

"A dependable nanny is what I need," Ryder said.

"Well, if you can get a sitter, I've got tickets to the Rangers game on Thursday. Take care, buddy," he said, rising from the couch and patting Ryder on the shoulder. "Keep the faith, bud. And move me up on that backup list. I'm more dependable than your Aunt Joanie. I bet she's always busy."

Ryder smiled despite himself. "You got it. Thanks. If I can find a sitter, I'll go to that game with you."

"I'll believe it when I see it. 'Night," Marshall said and loped out of the house.

Ryder sank farther into his chair, kicked off his shoes and propped his shoes onto the coffee table. He considered reaching for that beer, but drinking anything would require too much energy. Hearing the roar of the crowd and the occasional crack of the bat hitting the ball from the game on his flat-screen TV with surround system, he closed his eyes.

Making sure the twins were safe, taking care of his patients and covering for Dr. Walters were the most important things in his life, but he knew he needed help, especially with the twins. He'd never dreamed how difficult it would be to find dependable caretakers for the boys. His head began to pound. He could feel his blood pressure rising. Pinching the bridge of his nose, for one moment, he deliberately chose *not* to think about the next nanny he would need to hire and the deteriorating mental health of his mentor, Dr. Walters.

Ryder thought back to his high school days when he'd been catcher and Marshall had pitched. They'd won the state championship senior year. That weekend had been full of celebration. He remembered a cheerleader who had paid attention to him for the first time. She'd given him a night full of memories. Blonde, curvy and wiggly, she'd kept him busy. He hadn't lasted long the first time, but he'd done better the second and the third.

His lips tilted upward at the memory. He remembered the thrill of winning. There had never been a happier moment in his life. He sighed, and the visual of a different woman filled his mind. She had dark shoulder-length hair with a wicked red mouth and cool blue eyes. She wore a black dress that handled her curves the same way a man would. She would be a seductive combination of soft and firm with full breasts and inviting hips. She would kiss him into insanity and make him want more. He would slide his hands into her feminine wetness and make her gasp, then make her gasp again when he thrust inside her….

Ryder blinked. He was brick-hard and his heart was racing as if he were having sex. He swore out loud.

He couldn't believe himself. Maybe Marshall was right. Maybe he just really needed to get laid. His only problem was that the woman in his daydream had been

Problem Princess Bridget Devereaux. Yep, Marshall was right. Ryder was a nut job.

Bridget read Dr. Ryder McCall's dossier for the hundredth time in three days. He hadn't had the easiest upbringing in the world. His father had died when he was eight years old. His mother had died two years ago.

Ryder had played baseball in high school and won an academic scholarship. He'd graduated first in his college class, then first in his medical-school class.

His older brother, Cory, had played football and earned a college scholarship. Unfortunately, he was injured, so he dropped out, took a job as a department-store manager and married his high-school sweetheart. They'd waited to have children. Six months after the birth of twin boys, they'd attended an anniversary dinner but never made it home. A tractor trailer jackknifed in front of them on the freeway. They both died before they arrived at the emergency room.

An unbelievable tragedy. Even though Bridget had lost both her parents within years of each other, she had never been close to them. Ryder had clearly been close to his brother. Now, a man who had previously been unswervingly focused on his studies and career, was alone with those precious motherless babies.

Her heart broke every time she read his story. This was one of those times she wished she had a magic wand that would solve all of Ryder's problems and heal his pain. But she didn't. As much as she wished it were true, Bridget was all too certain of her humanity.

In the midst of all of this, she still had a job to do. She needed to bring doctors to Chantaine, and Dr. McCall's assistant hedged every time Bridget attempted to make an appointment. She would give the assistant two more tries, then Bridget would face Ryder in his own territory. If he thought an assistant would keep her at bay, he had no concept of her will. Surprise, surprise, especially to herself. She may have portrayed an airy, charming personality, but underneath it all, she was growing a backbone.

Chapter Two

Ryder left the hospital and picked up the boys after the latest sitter unexpectedly informed him that her child had a medical appointment she could not skip. He had an important meeting with several members of the hospital board this afternoon which *he* could not skip. He hated to press his admin assistant into baby service again, but it couldn't be helped.

After wrestling the boys in and out of car seats and the twin stroller, he felt like he'd run a 10K race as he pushed the stroller into his office suite. Instantly noting that his admin assistant was absent from her desk, he felt his stomach twist with dread. She'd left her desk tidy and organized as usual. She'd also left a note on his desk. He snatched it up and read it.

Miss Bridget Devereaux called 3x this a.m. I can't put her off forever. Gone to my anniversary celebration as discussed. Thank you for letting me off.

—Maryann

Ryder swore out loud then remembered the boys were in the room with him. "Don't ever say that word," he told them. "Bad word."

He recalled Maryann asking for the afternoon off—it had to have been a week or so ago. He'd been busy when she asked and hadn't given it a second thought. Now, he had to juggle his boys and an important meeting. He shook his head. Women managed children and careers all the time. Why was it so difficult for him? He was a healthy, intelligent man. He'd run marathons, worked more than twenty-four hours straight, brought a man back to life in the E.R., but taking care of these boys made him feel like a train wreck.

Ryder sat down at his desk and flipped through his contact list on his computer for someone he could call to watch the boys during his meeting. He sent a few emails and made three calls. All he got were voice mails.

"Well, hello, Phantom Man," a feminine voice called from the doorway.

Ryder swallowed an oath. Just what he needed right now. He didn't even need to look to know it was *Princess Persistent*. But he did and couldn't deny that she was a sight for sore eyes. Wearing another black dress, although this one looked a slight bit more like business wear, she smiled at him with that wicked red mouth that reminded him of what he hadn't had in a long time.

Dismissing the thought, he lifted his hand. "I have no time to talk. Important meeting in less than—" He glanced at the clock. "Thirty minutes. Got to find some-one one to watch the boys."

"Not having any luck?" she asked.

"No."

"You sound desperate," she said, sympathy lacking in her tone.

"Not desperate," he said. "Pressed."

"Oh, well as soon as you give me a time for our meeting, I'll get out of your way."

"I already told you I don't have time," he said in a voice that no one in their right mind would question.

She shrugged. "All I want is for you to pull up your calendar and ink me in," she said. "You already agreed."

"Not—"

She crossed her arms over her chest. "You have your job. I have mine."

Travis arched against the stroller restraints as if he wanted out. The baby wore an expression of displea-sure, which would soon turn to defiance and fury, which would also include unpleasant sound effects. Ryder loos-ened the strap and pulled him into his arms.

Tyler looked up expectantly and began the same arch-ing action against the stroller. Ryder withheld an oath.

"Want some help?" Bridget asked.

"Yes," he said. "If you could hold Tyler, I have one more person I can—" He stopped as he watched her settle the baby on her hip. An idea sprang to mind. "Can you keep them for an hour or so?"

Her eyes widened in alarm. "An hour?" she echoed. "Or so?"

"Just for this meeting," he said. "I'll leave as soon as possible."

She shot him a considering look. "In exchange for an opportunity to discuss Chantaine's medical proposition with you, and you having an *open mind*."

"I agree to the first half. The second is going to be tough."

"How tough would it be to take your twins to your important meeting?" she challenged.

The woman was playing dirty. "Okay," he said. "As long as you understand, my first priority is my residents' professional success."

"Done," she said. "Did you bring a blanket and some food?"

"Whatever the sitter keeps in the diaper bag," he said, relief flowing through him like a cool stream of water. "Thank you," he said, setting Travis in the stroller seat. "I'll see you after the meeting," he said and closed the office door behind him.

Bridget stared at the babies and they stared at her. Travis began to wiggle and make a frown face.

"Now, don't you start," she said, pointing her finger at him. "You haven't even given me a chance." She set Tyler in the other stroller seat and dove into the diaper bag and struck gold. "A blanket," she said. "You're going to love this," she said and spread it on the floor. Afterward, she set Travis on the blanket, followed by Tyler.

The boys looked at her expectantly.

"What?" she asked. "You're free from the bondage of the stroller. Enjoy yourselves." She narrowed her eyes. "Just don't start crawling or anything. Okay? Let's see what else is in the bag."

Unfortunately, not much. She used up the small

container of Cheerios within the first fifteen minutes and fifteen minutes after that, both boys had lost interest in the small set of blocks. She pulled out a musical toy and helped them work that over for several minutes.

Peekaboo killed a few more minutes, but then Bridget started to feel a little panicky. She needed more snacks and toys if she was going to keep the little darlings entertained. Grabbing some blank paper from Ryder's desk, she gave each boy a sheet.

Travis immediately put it in his mouth.

"Let's try something else," she said and crumpled the paper.

He smiled as if he liked the idea. Great, she thought. More paper. She crumpled a few sheets into a ball and tossed it at them. They loved that. They threw paper all over the room.

After a few more minutes, Travis began to fuss, stuffing his fist in his mouth.

"Hungry?" It would help so much if they could tell her what they needed. Luckily two bottles were also stuffed in the bag. She pulled out one and began to feed Travis. Tyler's face crumpled and he began to cry.

"Great, great," she muttered and awkwardly situated both boys on her lap as she fed them both their bottles.

They drained them in no time. Travis burped on her dress.

Bridget grimaced. A second later, Tyler gave her the same favor.

At least they weren't crying, she thought, but then she sniffed, noticing an unpleasant odor. A quick check revealed Travis had left a deposit in his diaper.

* * *

Ryder opened the door to his office prepared for screaming, crying, accusations from Bridget. Instead the boys were sprawled across her lap while she sang a medical magazine to the tune of *Frère Jacques*. He had to admit it was pretty inventive. His office looked like a disaster zone with papers strewn everywhere and he smelled the familiar, distinct scent of dirty diapers. He must have wrinkled his nose.

She did the same. "I didn't think it would be considerate to toss the diapers into the hallway, so they're in the trash can. I bundled them up as best as I could."

The boys looked safe and content. That was what was important. "It looks like you had a good time."

"Not bad," she said with a smile. "Considering my resources. You're really not set up for babies here."

"I can't agree more," he said and snatched up a few wads of paper. "What were you doing?"

"Playing ball with paper. It worked until Travis was determined to eat it." She gingerly lifted one of the boys in Ryder's direction. "So, when do we have our discussion?"

He tucked Tyler into the stroller and followed with Travis. Ryder was tempted to name a time next year but knew that wouldn't be fair. Better to get it over with. "Tonight, at my house," he said. "Do you like Chinese?"

"I prefer Italian or Mediterranean," she said, frowning as she rose to her feet. "At your house?"

"It's the one and only time I can guarantee for the foreseeable future."

She sighed. "It's not what I hoped for. How am I going to have your undivided attention?"

"Maybe we'll get lucky and they'll go to sleep," he said.

Four hours later, Bridget could barely remember what she'd said or eaten for dinner. The boys had taken a nap in the car on the way home and woken up cranky. She suspected they hadn't gotten enough of an afternoon nap. Although she resented the fact that she wasn't getting Ryder's undivided attention during their discussion, she couldn't really blame him. In fact, despite the fact that he was clearly a strong man, she could tell that caring for the twins was wearing on him. He loved them and would protect them with his life, but the man needed consistent help.

It was close to eleven before the twins truly settled down.

"I'd offer you a ride to wherever you're staying, but I can't pull the boys out of bed again," he said, after he had made the trip up and down the stairs five times.

His eyes filled with weariness, he raked a hand through his hair. Her heart tugged at his quandary. The urge to help, to fix, was overwhelming. "My security is always close by. He can collect me. It's no problem."

"I keep forgetting you're a princess," he said.

"Maybe it's the baby formula on my dress," she said drily.

"Maybe," he said, meeting her gaze. The moment swelled between them.

Bridget felt her chest grow tight and took a breath to alleviate the sensation.

"I'm sure you're tired. You could stay here if you want," he offered. "I have a guest room and bath."

Bridget blinked. She *was* tired, but staying here? "I don't have a change of clothes."

He shrugged. "I can give you a shirt to sleep in."

The prospect of sleeping in Ryder's shirt was wickedly seductive. Plus, she *was* tired. "I'd like to get your nanny situation in order for you."

"That would be a dream come true," he said. "Everything I've done so far hasn't worked."

"There may be a fee for an agency," she said. "I'm not sure how it works here. I'll have to ask my sister."

"I took the first and second suggestions that were given to me and they didn't pan out. It's imperative that I have excellent care for the boys. "

"I can see that," she said. "But do you also realize that you will have to make some adjustments as time goes on? Later, there will be sports and school activities where parents are expected to attend." Bridget remembered that neither of her parents had attended her school activities. Occasionally a nanny had shown up, but never her parents. "Have you figured out how you'll address that?"

He frowned thoughtfully. "I haven't figured out much. I haven't had custody very long. It's still a shock to all of us. I know the boys miss their mother and father, but they can't express it. I hate the loss for them. And I'm not sure I'm such a great choice as a parent. I've been totally dedicated to my career since I entered med school. Add to that how I've been filling in for Dr. Walters and it's tough. I don't want to let down my residents or the twins."

Bridget studied Ryder for a long moment. "Are you

sure you want to step in as their father? There are other options. There are people who would love to welcome the boys into their—"

"The boys are mine," he said, his jaw locking in resolution. "It may take me some time, but I'll figure it out. The boys are important to me. I held them minutes after they were born. I would do anything for them. We've just all been thrown a loop. We're all dealing with the loss of my brother and sister-in-law. I will be there for them. I will be."

She nodded slowly. "Okay. I'll try to help you with your nanny situation."

He paused and the electricity and emotion that flowed between them snapped and crackled. "Thank you."

She nodded. "It's late. I may need to borrow one of your shirts and I should talk to my security."

"No problem," he said, but the way he looked at her made her feel as if he'd much prefer she share his bed instead of taking the guest bed alone.

Bridget took a quick shower and brushed her teeth with the toothbrush Ryder supplied. Pushing her hands through the sleeves of the shirt he left in the guest bedroom for her, she drank in the fresh scent of the shirt. She climbed into bed, wondering what had possessed her to get involved in Ryder's situation and she remembered all the things she couldn't control or influence. Maybe, just maybe she could wave a magic wand in this one and help just a little.

It seemed only seconds after she fell asleep that she heard a knock at the door. She awakened, confused and disoriented. "Hello?"

"Bridget," a male voice said from the other side of the door. "It's me, Ryder."

The door opened a crack. “I just wanted you to know I’m leaving.”

Her brain moved slowly. She was not at the hotel. She was at Ryder’s townhome. “Um.”

“The boys are still asleep.”

She paused. “The boys?” She blinked. “Oh, the boys.”

He came to the side of her bed. “Are you okay?”

“What time is it?”

“Five a.m.”

“Is this when you usually leave for work?”

“Pretty much,” he said.

“Okay,” she said and tried to make her brain work. “What time do they usually get up?”

“Six or seven,” he said. “I can try and call someone if—”

“No, I can do it,” she said. “Just leave my door open so I can hear them.”

“Are you sure?”

“Yes. Check in at lunchtime,” she said.

“I can do that,” he said and paused. “Did anyone ever tell you how beautiful you are when you’re half-asleep?”

Unconsciously, her mouth lifted in a half smile. “I can’t recall such a compliment.”

“Nice to know I’m the first,” he said, bending toward her and pressing his mouth against hers. Before she could say a word, he left.

Bridget wondered if she’d dreamed the kiss.

She fell back asleep for what must have been 30 seconds and she heard the sound of a baby’s cry. It awakened her like cold water on her face. She sat upright, climbed out of bed and walked to the boys’ room. She swung open the door to find Travis and Tyler sitting in their cribs and wailing.

"Hi, darlings," she said and went to Travis. "Good morning. It's a wonderful day to be a baby, isn't it?" She saw a twisty thing on the side of the crib and cranked it around. The mobile turned and music played. "Well, look at that," she said and touched the mobile.

Travis gave a few more sobs, but as soon as he looked upward, he quieted as the mobile turned.

Bridget felt a sliver of relief. "Good boy," she said and went to Tyler's bed and cranked up the mobile. Tyler looked upward and gave up his halfhearted cry, staring at the mobile.

Diaper change, she thought and took care of Travis. Then she took care of Tyler and hoisted both boys on her hips and went downstairs. She fed them, changed them again and propped them on a blanket in the den while she called her sister's friend for a reference for the best nanny agency in Dallas. Three hours later, she interviewed four nannies in between feeding the twins and changing more diapers and putting them down for a nap. When they fussed at nap time, she played a CD more repetitious than her brother's top-adviser's speech on a royal's duty. She'd heard that lecture too many times to count. The huge advantage to the babies' CD was that it included singing. Bridget wondered if she might have been more receptive to the lecture if the adviser had sung it.

The second prospective nanny was her favorite. She received letters of reference on her cell phone within an hour and sent a generous offer that was immediately accepted. After she checked on the boys, she ordered a nanny/babycam. Next in line, she would hire a relief nanny, but right now she needed a little relief of her own.

Bridget sank onto the couch and wondered when her day had felt so full. Even at this moment, she needed to use the bathroom, but she didn't have the energy to go. She glanced at herself, in her crumpled dress from yesterday with baby formula, baby food and liquid baby burp. That didn't include the drool.

Crazy, but the drool was sweet to her. How sick was that? But she knew the twins had drooled when they'd relaxed and trusted her.

She laughed quietly, a little hysterically. Anyone in their right mind would ask why she was working so hard to find a nanny for a doctor with two baby boys. Maybe a shrink could explain it, but these days, Bridget had a hard time turning down a cause of the heart. And Ryder and the boys had struck her straight in the heart with a deadly aim. She hoped, now, that she would feel some sort of relief.

Leaning back against the sofa with her bladder a little too full, she closed her eyes. Heaven help her, this baby stuff was exhausting.

Ryder left the office early, determined not to leave Bridget totally in the lurch with the boys. Stepping inside the front door, he found Bridget, mussed in the most alluring way, asleep on his couch.

She blinked, then her eyes widened. "Oh, excuse me. Just a second," she said, then raced down the hallway.

He listened carefully, automatically these days. A CD played over the baby monitor, but there were no other sounds. A double check never hurt, he thought, and strode upstairs to listen outside the nursery door.

Nothing. He opened the doorknob in slow motion and pushed the door open. Carefully stepping inside, he peeked into the cribs. Both boys were totally zoned out. He almost wondered if they were snoring but refused to check.

Backing out of the room, he returned downstairs to the den. Bridget was sipping from a glass of water.

"Are they still asleep?" she asked.

He nodded.

She grimaced. "I hate to say this. You have no idea how much I hate to say this, but we need to wake them or they'll be up all night. And I'm not staying tonight."

"Yeah," he said, but he was in no rush.

"I hired a nanny. She can start Monday. I've also ordered a baby/nannycam for your peace of mind. The next step is hiring a relief nanny because the twins are especially demanding at this age. Well, maybe they will be demanding at every age, but we have to deal with the present and the immediate future."

Ryder stared at her in disbelief. "How did you do that?"

She smiled. "I'm a fairy princess. I waved my magic wand," she said. "Actually I got into the best nanny agency in Dallas, used my title, interviewed four highly qualified women in between changing diapers, selected one applicant, received references, blah, blah, blah and it's done." She lifted her shoulders. "And now I'm done."

"I'm sure you are. In any other circumstance, I would invite you out to dinner for the evening."

"Lovely thought," she said. "But I feel extremely grungy. The opposite of glamorous. I'm going to my sister's ranch for the weekend. You can call me next week about all the doctors you want to send to Chantaine."

His lips twitched. "You don't really think I'm going to sell out one of my residents for this, do you?"

"Sell out is such a harsh term," she said with a scowl. "I believe it's more accurate that you're giving them an opportunity for hands-on experience in a beautiful environment with a compensation that allows them to concentrate on treatment rather than their debt."

He lifted an eyebrow. "Pretty good."

She shrugged. "It's the truth. My security is waiting to drive me to my sister's house. Can you take it from here?"

"Yes, I can. Do I have your number?" he asked. "For that dinner I promised."

She looked at him for a long, sexy moment that made him want to find a way to make her stay. "Some would say I'm more trouble than I'm worth," she said.

"They haven't seen you with twins," he said.

She smiled slightly and went to the kitchen. Out of curiosity, he followed and watched her scratch a number across the calendar tacked on the fridge. "Good enough?" she asked.

"Good enough," he said.

"Don't wait too long to call me, cowboy doctor," she said and walked toward the front door.

"I won't," he said, his gaze fixed on the sight of her amazing backside. "G'night, gorgeous."

She tossed a smile over her shoulder. "Same to you."

Bridget felt Valentina search her face. "Twin boys? Dr. Ryder? What does any of this have to do with you?"

It was Saturday morning. Noon, actually, as she sipped her tea and entered the world of the waking. "I didn't mean to get involved, but I didn't have a choice. I mean, the boys were orphaned. Ryder is grieving at the same time he's trying to take care of the babies. Trying to take on someone else's job because he's medically unable."

Tina stared at her in disbelief. "Are you sure you're okay? Maybe you need more rest."

Bridget laughed. "I'm sure I'll take another nap, but the story won't change tomorrow. It was something I had to do." She paused. "You understand that, don't you? When you have to fix it if you can?"

Tina's face softened and she covered Bridget's hand with hers. "Oh, sweetie, I'm so sorry," she said, shaking her head.

"For what?"

"The Devereaux fixing gene has kicked in," she said. "It's a gift and a plague."

"What do you mean?"

"I mean, you finally understand what it means to be a Devereaux Royal," she said, her expression solemn. "If you see a need, you try to fill it. If you see a pain, you try to heal it. It's your purpose. It's our purpose."

"So, I'm going to be doing stuff like this the rest of my life?" Bridget asked, appalled.

Tina nodded and Katiana banged on the tray of her high chair, clearly wanting more food.

"Oh, I hope not." Bridget didn't want to feel that much. She didn't want to get that emotionally involved. Surely, she could get this out of her system once and for all with Ryder and the babies and then get back to her true self in Italy.

Bridget sighed. "What I really want to do is wrap up

this doctor thing as soon as possible. I'm concerned it may not happen as quickly as I like."

"Why not?" Tina asked as she gave Katiana slices of peaches.

"I don't understand it all, but the way Ryder talks about it, going to Chantaine would be death for a physician's career. Sounds a bit overdramatic to me, but I need to get further information. In the meantime, Stefan has asked me to make some more official appearances, so I'll be traveling and spending more time in Dallas."

Tina frowned. "I don't like that," she said. "I thought you were going to spend most of your time here with me."

"I'll still be coming to the ranch as often as possible, but you know how Stefan is. He likes to maximize our efforts."

"How well I remember," Tina said with a groan. She dampened a clean cloth and wiped off Katiana's face and hands.

Katiana shook her adorable head and lifted her hands. "Up," she said.

"Of course, Your Highness," Tina said and gave her daughter a kiss as she lifted her from the chair.

Katiana immediately pointed at the floor. "Down."

"Please," Tina said.

Katiana paused.

"Please," Tina repeated. "Can you say that?"

"Psss," the toddler said.

"Close enough," Tina said with a laugh.

Bridget stared at her sister in jeans and a T-shirt and sometimes had to shake her head at the sight of her. "I'm just not used to seeing you quite so domesticated."

"I've been living here for more than two years now."

"Do you mind it? The work?" she asked. "At the palace, you could have had several nannies at your beck and call."

"I have Hildie the housekeeper, who may as well be Katiana's grandmother, and Zach. I like the simplicity of this life. Before I met Zach, I always felt like I was juggling a dozen priorities. Now between him and Katiana, the choice is easy."

"Must be nice," Bridget muttered as Hildie, Zach's longtime housekeeper, strode through the door carrying a bag of groceries.

"Well, hello, all Your Highlinesses. We've got a roomful of royalty today. Miss Tina, did you offer your sister some of that strawberry bread? Looks like you're having a late breakfast. Although that should come as no surprise considering when she got here last night," Hildie said, lifting her eyebrow.

Bridget wasn't quite certain how to take the stern-looking gray-haired woman. Tina insisted the woman had a heart of gold, but she seemed to rule the house with an iron hand. "Good morning, Miss—"

"Call me Hildie, and it's afternoon. Do you feel like some pancakes or a turkey sandwich? You looked pretty rough when you got in last night," Hildie said as she began to put away groceries.

"She was taking care of twin babies," Tina said, clearly still amazed.

Hildie's jaw dropped. "Twin babies," she said. "You?"

Bridget grimaced. "I know it's totally improbable. Hopefully I won't be put in that type of situation again."

"She was helping a doctor who had become a

guardian to his brother's two babies because the brother and sister-in-law were killed in an accident."

Hildie shook her head, her brow furrowing in deep sympathy. "That's terrible, just terrible. You did the right thing," she said to Bridget. "Let me fix you a pie. I'll fix you any kind you want."

Surprised, Bridget felt a rush of discomfort mixed with pleasure. "Oh, I don't need a pie. You're delightful to suggest it, but—"

"I insist," Hildie said.

Tina lifted her shoulders helplessly. "You're going to get a pie whether you like it or not. You may as well pick what you like, and I guarantee it will be the best pie you've eaten."

"Well, if you must, I would like the most decadent chocolate pie you can bake."

Hildie cackled with laughter. "Chocolate. You can tell the two of you are sisters. And you may try to hide it, but you have that fix-it compulsion just like your sister."

"I don't have that compulsion," Bridget insisted. "It's temporary. Like a virus. As soon as I take my long break in Italy, I'll be cured."

Hildie laughed again and shot her a look of sympathy. "Don't worry, Your Highliness. It may take a while, but you'll figure it out."

Bridget frowned because it seemed that Hildie knew something she didn't. Hmm. The prospect didn't please her, but the chocolate would help.

Chapter Three

Three nights later, Ryder met Bridget at an exclusive Mediterranean restaurant in Dallas. He remembered she'd said she preferred Mediterranean and Italian food. With the Dallas skyline outside the window beside them, he couldn't look anywhere but at her. Her blue eyes sparkled with a combination of sensuality and warmth. Her black dress—yet another one—dipped into a V that cupped her beautiful breasts and her lips were, again, red.

"Thank you for joining me," he said after they'd placed their order.

"Thank you for inviting me. Who's watching the twins?" she asked.

"A neighbor and her daughter. I'm paying double. Amazing how easy it was for them to commit when I said that," he said.

She laughed. "They're adorable but exhausting. How was the new nanny?"

"Scary efficient. This was her first day and she's already whipping all of us into shape," he said, amazed at how good he felt just to be with Bridget.

"Good. Next step is to get a backup," she said and took a sip of wine. "In the meantime, about Chantaine's medical program…"

He stifled a groan. "Do we have to discuss business?"

"Briefly," she said and lifted an eyebrow. "Remember that we held our discussion while the twins were screaming *after* I had cared for them during your meeting and—"

"Okay, okay," he said. "Do you want me to be blunt?"

"I would love it," she said, leaning forward and propping her chin on her hands.

"The truth is, there's no true professional advantage for the residents to go to Chantaine after they graduate. There's no extra education, association with an expert, or certification."

"So money is not enough," she said.

"No," he said.

"Hmm." She tilted her head. "So the whole game would change if Chantaine could offer exposure to a noted expert in a particular field?"

He nodded.

She took another sip of her wine. "Thank you."

He could tell her brain was already racing. "You're plotting and planning," he said.

She smiled, her sexy red lips lifting upward, sending a sensual heat through his veins. "Yes, I am. I'll figure something out. It's the Devereaux way."

"I did an internet search on you," he admitted. "You've *mostly* stayed out of trouble. How did you manage that?"

"I'm flattered. Of course, I did research on you right after the cocktail party. How did I stay out of trouble?" she asked. "It's all relative. My sisters did me a huge favor. I wouldn't wish it on her, but Ericka went to rehab, and then after that, Tina got pregnant. What a scandal. So my little tumbles—"

"Like the time you got smashed at the nightclub in Chantaine and made a scene—"

"That was Stefan's fault. Eve was with me and he couldn't stand the fact that she wasn't with him." She waved her hand. "But I won't fault him too much. He'd just discovered he had a baby from an earlier affair and was trying to work out his relationship with Eve."

"I remember reading an article about some sort of incident. A gang. She was hurt."

He stopped when he saw her gaze darken with emotion.

"She saved my life and nearly lost her own," Bridget said quietly as she ran her finger around the top of her glass. "It all happened so fast. I wish I had responded differently. She was hurt. She almost died." She lifted her glass and took a quick sip. "It was wrong. Her life shouldn't have been put in jeopardy for my sake."

He was shocked at the stark guilt he saw on her face. "These things happen. Decisions are made in microseconds. She's a Texas girl. She acted on instinct."

She bit her lip. "Maybe I need to learn some of those Texas-girl instincts," she muttered.

"Your instincts are pretty damn good. You took care of the twins when we were in a jam," he said.

"That's different," she said.

"Not as far as I can see. I won't lie to you. I can't make any promises about sending doctors to Chantaine. On the other hand, I've thought about having you in my bed way too much. I wish I could say it's just because you've got a killer body and I've done without, but the truth is, there's something else about you that gets me going."

Her lips parted in startled disbelief. "I—" She broke off and shook her head. "I don't know what to say."

"You don't have to say anything. I just wanted you to know," he said.

She met his gaze and he could tell she was undecided. He saw want and hesitation, and he understood it, but he was driven to find a way to get her to meet him halfway.

After a delicious dinner, Ryder drove Bridget to her hotel and insisted on walking her to her room. "You know security is watching me," she said as they stood outside her door.

"Do you want to step inside your room?"

An illicit thrill raced through her. Her guard would report to Stefan and he would fuss. She would dodge his calls the same way she had after spending the night at Ryder's house. What a hassle. "For just a moment," she said and slid her key card into the lock.

Ryder pushed open the door. Seconds later, she felt her back against the door and his mouth on hers.

"Do you know what your red mouth does to me?"

he muttered and plundered her lips. He slid his tongue into her mouth, tasting her, taking her.

Her heart slammed against her ribs. She couldn't resist the urge to lift her fingers to his hair and scalp.

He groaned in approval and rocked his hips against hers.

Bridget gasped, her breath locking somewhere between her lungs and throat. Somehow, someway, she craved his warmth and strength. His passion and need struck her at her core.

"I want you," he said. "You want me. Let me stay for a while."

A terrible wicked temptation rolled through her. If he stayed, he would fill her and take her away from her uncertainty and emptiness. She knew he could take care of her, if only for a little while.

He French-kissed her, sending her around the world at least a couple of times.

"You want me to stay?" he asked, sliding his mouth down over her ear.

She inhaled, grasping for sanity. Closing her eyes, she tried to concentrate. "Yesandno," she said, running the words together. She dipped her head so that her forehead rested against his chin. "This is a little fast."

He gave a heavy, unsatisfied sigh. "Yeah, it is. But it's strong."

She nodded. "Sorry," she whispered.

"It's okay," he said cradling the back of her head. "It wouldn't work out anyway."

"Why is that?" she asked, leaning back to look at him.

"I'm a doctor. You're a princess," he said.

"So?" she asked.

"The two don't mix," he said. "And never will. Sweet dreams, Your Highness."

He left and Bridget stared at the door, frowning. *Why couldn't they mix?* Not that she *wanted* them to mix. And the *sweet dreams* thing really grated on her. That was what Eve had often said. It had seemed so sweet when she'd said it. Not so with Ryder. Bridget snarled. He was gone. Good riddance.

Ryder heard a knocking sound and shook his head as he glanced up during the meeting he was in to discuss the performance of the residents.

Dr. Wayne Hutt, Ryder's nemesis, knocked on the table again. "Dr. McCall?" he said. "Anyone home?"

"Pardon me," Ryder said in a crisp voice. "I was studying my notes."

"Apology accepted," Hutt said. "Drs. Robinson and Graham are having attendance issues."

"Dr. Robinson is concerned about the welfare of his family in rural Virginia and Dr. Graham's wife has just gotten pregnant," Ryder said. "They just need a little time to refocus. It won't be a problem."

"How can you be sure?" Hutt challenged.

Ryder fought his antipathy for his associate. "I'm sure," he said. "Just as Dr. Gordon Walters would be sure," he said, pulling rank because everyone knew Dr. Walters trusted Ryder over anyone else.

Hutt gave an odd combination of a frown and grimace.

Dr. James Williams, chief of everything, nodded.

"We'll give these two interns two weeks to make adjustments. Dr. McCall, you'll speak to them?"

"Yes, sir."

Seven minutes later, the meeting ended, thank God. He returned to his office and sent emails to Drs. Robinson and Graham to set up appointments. He answered another fifty emails and stood to make late rounds with his patients.

A knock sounded outside his door and Dr. Hutt walked inside. "Hey, Ryder. Late night. I'm surprised you can do this with the twins."

Ryder resisted the urge to grind his teeth. "I've hired a new nanny and am getting new backup. Thanks for your concern. I need to do late rounds."

"Just a minute," Hutt said. "How's Dr. Walters doing? No one's talking."

"He's working through his recovery. These things take time," Ryder hedged.

"That's pretty vague," Hutt said.

"You know I can't discuss the confidential status of patients," he said.

"But Walters isn't really your patient," Hutt continued.

"He's my mentor and friend, the closest thing I've had to a father since my own father died when I was a kid. I'm not discussing his condition," Ryder said.

"It must not be good," Hutt said. "You know if the twins are too much for you, I'll be glad to step in and help."

Ryder just bet Hutt would like to step in and *help.* What Hutt really wanted was a promotion. What Hutt really wanted was to snatch Walters's position away from Ryder. Although Ryder hated that Walters couldn't fulfill his duties any longer.

"Thanks for the offer," he said.

"Seriously, Ryder. I have a wife and a child. The wife is the critical element. She makes it easy for me to do my job. When you don't have a wife..."

"I have a good new nanny," he said.

"It's not the same as a wife," Hutt counseled.

"Hmm. See you. Good night," he said and headed out the door. What Hutt didn't understand was that Ryder had never had any intention of getting married and having children. He'd observed his parents' disastrous marriage, his father's death and his mother's subsequent descent into alcoholism and death.

After that, Ryder had resolved that he wanted to heal people. Bag the personal relationships, with the exception of his brother and his family. His family became his patients, and after he completed his residency, his family included the new residents. And always Dr. Walters. He would never take a wife. His mind wandered to a visual of Bridget the last time he'd seen her, her eyes catlike with sensuality, her mouth soft and sensual, taking him into her. His mouth into her. When he really wanted to give her a lot more.

Ryder swore under his breath. This was all libido. He'd taken care of this issue before with other women doctors as career-driven as he was. No-ties sex provided a release that allowed him to do his job. Maintaining his focus on his profession and the twins was the most important thing. Bridget was just a distraction.

Bridget wandered around the medical association meeting and was bummed that Ryder wasn't there. He was probably taking care of the twins. She felt a deep tug of sympathy and quickly tried to brush it aside. Ryder didn't want her sympathy. They would never work. Remember? She covered her irritation with a smile as she nodded at someone else she didn't know.

Halfway through the evening, the shrimp bowl was refilled and Bridget put a few on her plate.

"I always wait for the refill at these things," a distinguished older man said to her.

She nodded in agreement. "I agree. Fresh is better. Bridget Devereaux," she said, extending her free hand.

"Dr. James Williams, University Hospital," he said shaking her hand. "Are you a pharmaceutical sales rep?"

She opened her mouth and it took a moment to speak. She smiled. "Not exactly. I'm representing the country of Chantaine. Very small country in the Mediterranean. We're trying to recruit more doctors. We're offering complimentary living expenses and paying special scholarships in addition to salary for a two-year stay."

Dr. Williams lifted his white eyebrows. "Really? I'll have to speak to my physician in charge of residents about that. Perhaps a couple of them could benefit from that."

"I would appreciate that very much. I'm sure you're a very busy man. Would you mind if I touch base with you in a week or so?"

"Not at all," he said. "Some of our residents have money challenges. Don't we all in this economy?"

"So true," she said. "Are you the speaker tonight?"

He shook his head. "No, I'm lucky. Eat and leave."

She laughed. "Don't rub it in," she said.

He laughed in return. “Tell me your name again. I don’t want to forget.”

“Bridget Devereaux,” she said, deliberately leaving out her title. “I represent Chantaine. I’m honored to meet you.”

“My pleasure to meet you, Miss Devereaux,” he said, and ate his shrimp cocktail.

Bridget worked the room the rest of the night and arranged a visit to the pediatric wing at Texas Medical Center to make a public service announcement for public health. She also met several doctors who wanted to pursue a more personal relationship, but she demurred at the same time that she gave them her card which contained a number for her assistant.

By the time the evening was done, her feet were also done. Her mind wandered to Ryder and the babies, but she tried to push her thoughts aside. With a glass of white wine in her hand, she kicked off her high heels and watched television in her suite at the hotel.

She closed her eyes. Soon enough she would be in Italy with a gorgeous Italian man keeping her company. She smiled at the image, but soon another image flashed in its place. Ryder, sans shirt, stood before her and dragged her into his arms and began to make love to her. He was so hot that smoke rose between them, but the sensation of his skin against hers made her dizzy. His kiss made her knees weak. He made her want in a way she never had….

She felt herself sinking into the couch, her body warm and pliable. And alone.

Bridget blinked and sat up against the couch. This was just wrong. He’d already said they wouldn’t work because of who he was, because of who she was. A part of her rebelled against the notion one moment. The next, she didn't. She didn't have room for this drama in her life. She had goals. She had Italy in her future.

Bridget washed her face and brushed her teeth, determined to put Ryder from her mind. As she fell asleep, though, she dreamed of Ryder and the boys.

A few days later, Ryder followed up on a surgery patient midday. The young man had been admitted to the E.R. with appendicitis. Ryder had operated and needed to give his stamp of approval for the teen to be discharged. He was stopped because there was filming in the pediatric unit.

Slightly irritated, he checked his text messages on his cell and answered a few.

"She's a princess making a video," one nurse said to another.

He snapped his head up at the comment. "Princess?" he repeated.

"Yes," the nurse said. "But she's very nice. Not at all snooty. I got her coffee and she was very grateful. More than a lot of doctors."

"She wasn't trying to save lives," Ryder said.

The nurse shrugged. "Anyone can say please and thank you, and she did."

Minutes later, Bridget appeared, lighting up the room with her smile. The chief of Pediatrics accompanied her, clearly dazzled.

"Thank you," she said. "Thank you so much from Chantaine and me. You have been wonderful."

"Isn't she wonderful? Now *that* is a princess," the nurse said.

Ryder wanted to make a wry, cynical response, but he was too busy staring at Bridget. And the damned pediatric chief. She seemed to glow. He remembered how she'd felt in his arms, how that wicked red mouth had felt against his. He remembered how she'd made him smile. Not many people had managed to do that during the last few months.

She squeezed the pediatrics chief's arm, then glanced around the room and waved. Her gaze locked with his and he felt a surge of need all the way down to his feet. It was sexual, but more, and confused the hell out of him. She gave a quick little wave and returned her attention to the pediatric chief.

Ryder felt an inexplicable surge of jealousy. *Where the hell had that come from?* Pushing it aside, he continued to his patient's room for the final exam. Less than five minutes later, he headed down the hallway toward his office. Rounding a corner, he nearly plowed into Bridget and Dr. Ware, the pediatrics chief, who was chatting her up. His body language said he wanted to eat her with a spoon. His hand placed on the wall above her head, he leaned toward her. Ryder fought the crazy urge to push him away, but turned his head instead.

"Ryder. Dr. McCall," Bridget said.

He slowed his steps and turned around and nodded in her direction.

"How are you? The twins? The new nanny?" she asked, her gaze searching his.

Ware stepped beside her. "Whoa, she knows a lot about you, McCall. How did that happen?"

Ryder shrugged. "Just lucky, I guess. I'm good. The twins are good and the new nanny is fantastic. I could say I owe you my life, but I'd be afraid you'd take it."

She shot him a look of mock offense. "You know better than that. Besides, it's not your life that I want," she said with a laugh.

Ware looked from one of them to the other, clearly curious. "What *does* she want? And why in the world wouldn't you give it to her?"

"She wants my residents," he said, meeting her gaze.

"After they've completed your program," she insisted. "Plus, I only want to *borrow* them for a couple of years, and they'll be well compensated."

"You could throw her one or—" Dr. Ware's pager sounded. "Please excuse me. I need to go. You have my card, Your Highness. Give me a call. Anytime," he said with a hopeful smile and rushed away.

Bridget sighed and turned to Ryder. "Are you going to do the civilized thing and ask me to join you for lunch?"

"If I haven't been civilized before, why should I start now?" Ryder retorted because Bridget made him feel anything but civilized.

"I suppose because you owe me your life," she said with a glint in her eyes.

He gave a muffled chuckle. "Okay, come along. I better warn you that lunch won't last longer than fifteen minutes."

"Ah, so you're into quickies. What a shame," she said and began to walk.

"I didn't say that," he said, but resisted the urge to pull at his collar which suddenly felt too tight.

"I can't say I'm surprised. All evidence points in that direction."

"How did we get on this subject?" he asked.

"You said you wouldn't last more than fifteen minutes," she said, meeting his gaze with eyes so wide and guileless that he wondered how she did it.

"I said *lunch* won't last—" He broke when he saw her smile. "Okay, you got me on that one. I hope you don't mind cafeteria food."

"Not at all," she said as they walked into the cafeteria.

He noticed several people stared in their direction, but she seemed to ignore it. They each chose a couple dishes and he paid for both, then guided her to a less-occupied table at the back of the room. "How did your video go today?"

"Hopefully, well. I interviewed Dr. Ware about preventative health for children. I also need to do one for adults. But enough about that. How are the twins?" she asked, clearly eager for information.

"I think the new nanny is making a big difference for them. This is the most calm I've seen them since I took custody of them," he said. "The nanny also suggested that I do some extra activities with them, but I haven't worked that into the schedule yet."

"What kind of activities?" she asked, and took a bite of her chicken.

"Swimming," he said then lowered his voice. *"Baby yoga."*

"Oh. Do you take yoga?" she asked and sipped her hot tea.

"Never in my life," he said. "The nanny seems to

think this would increase bonding between the three of us."

"That makes you uncomfortable," she said.

He shrugged. "I hadn't planned on having kids. I guess I'm still adjusting, too."

"You've been through a lot. Perhaps you should see a therapist," she said.

"We're doing okay now," he said defensively.

"I don't suggest it as an insult. The palace is always giving us head checks especially since my sister Ericka had her substance-abuse problem. I'm surprised it's not required in this situation."

"A social worker has visited a few times to check on things. She actually suggested the same thing," he said reluctantly. "She said I need to make sure I'm having fun with the boys instead of it being all work."

"There you go," she said. "I think it's a splendid idea. You just seem incredibly overburdened and miserable."

"Thank you for that diagnosis, Your Highness," he said drily and dug into his dry salmon filet. "Funny, a friend of mine said something similar recently."

"We all have to protect against burnout. I would say you're more in danger of it than most."

"Is there such a thing as princess burnout?" he asked.

"Definitely. That's what happened to my sister Valentina. She carried the load too long."

"And what are you doing to prevent burnout?"

"I have an extended break planned in my future. In the meantime, I try to make sure I get enough rest and solitude whenever possible. As soon as I wrap up the doctor assignment, I'll get a break. I'm hoping you'll toss me one or two of your residents as Dr. Ware suggested to get the ball rolling."

"It's going to be more difficult than that," he said.

"I don't see why it needs to be. It's not as if I'm seriously asking for your top neurosurgeons. We would love a general practitioner or family doctor. In fact, we would prefer it."

"You and the rest of the world. We actually have a shortage of family physicians, too."

"Again, I'm only asking to *borrow* them."

"What do you think of Dr. Ware?" he asked, changing the subject again.

"He's lovely. Unlike you, he's totally enchanted with my position and title."

"Part of my charm. Part of the reason you find me irresistible."

"You flatter yourself," she said.

"Do I?" he challenged. "You've missed me."

"Of course I haven't. You already said nothing would work between us. Of course, that was after you tried to shag me against the hotel door. I mean, you obviously have the attention span of a fruit fly when it comes to women and—"

He closed his hand over hers. "Will you shut up for a minute?"

Surprisingly, she did.

"I dream about you whenever I get the rare opportunity to sleep. I've dialed your number and hung up too many times to count. You can't want to get involved with me right now."

"It's not for you to tell me what I can and can't want. Lord knows, everyone else does that. Don't you start."

"Okay," he said wearily.

"So what are you going to do about it?" she challenged.

If he said what he *wanted* to do, he could be arrested. "I think I'll show instead of tell," he said and watched with satisfaction as her throat and face bloomed with color. He wondered if her blush extended to the rest of her body. It would be fun to find out.

Chapter Four

Two days later, Bridget's cell phone rang and her heart went pitter-patter at the number on the caller ID.

"Hello," she said in a cool voice.

"Hello to you, Your Highness. How are you?" Ryder asked.

"I'm actually getting ready to make an appearance for a children's art program in Dallas," she said, smiling at the people who were waiting for her.

"Okay, I'll make this quick. Are you free tonight?"

She rolled her eyes. The man clearly had no idea how many demands were placed on her once people got word she was in the area. "I'm not often free but can sometimes make adjustments. What did you have in mind?"

"Swimming," he said.

"Excuse me?" she said.

"Swimming with the twins and pizza," he said.

"The pizza had better be fabulous. Ciao," she said and disconnected the call, but she felt a crazy surge of happiness zing through her as she followed the museum representatives inside the room where the children and press awaited.

Bridget gave a brief speech about the importance of art at all levels of society and dipped her hands and feet in purple paint. She stepped on a white sheet of paper, then pressed her handprints above and finished with her autograph.

The crowd applauded and she was technically done, but she stayed longer to talk to the children as they painted and worked on various projects. Their warmth and responsiveness made her feel less jaded, somehow less weary. Who would have thought it possible?

After extensive rearrangements of her schedule, Bridget put on her swimsuit and had second thoughts. What had possessed her to agree to join Ryder for a swim class when she was in a nearly naked state? She didn't have a perfectly slim body. In fact, if honest, she was curvy with pouches. Her bum was definitely larger than her top.

Her stomach clenched. Oh, bloody hell, she might as well be thirteen years old again. Forget it, she told herself. It wasn't as if anything could happen. She and Ryder would have two six-month-old chaperones.

Within forty-five minutes, she and Ryder stood in a pool with Tyler and Travis. Tyler stuck to her like glue, his eyes wide and fearful. "It's okay," she coaxed, bobbing gently in the water.

Ryder held Travis, who was screaming bloody murder.

"Are we having fun yet?" he asked, holding his godson securely.

"Should we sing?" she asked, trying not to be distracted by Ryder's broad shoulders and well-muscled arms and chest. For bloody's sake, when did the man have time to work out?

"They would throw us out," he said. "You look good in water."

She felt a rush of pleasure. "Thank you. Is Travis turning purple?"

"I think it's called rage," he said.

"Would you like to switch off for a moment?"

"Are you sure?" he asked doubtfully.

She nodded. "Let me give him a go," she said.

Tyler protested briefly at the exchange, then attached himself to Ryder. Travis continued to scream, so she lowered her mouth to his ear and began to quietly sing a lullaby from her childhood. Travis cried, but the sound grew less intense. She kept singing and he made sad little yelps, then finally quieted.

"Aren't you the magic one?" Ryder said.

"Luck," she said and cooed at the baby, swirling him around in the water. "Doesn't this feel good?" she murmured.

By the end of class, they'd switched off again and Travis was cackling and shrieking with joy as he splashed and kicked and Ryder whirled him around in the water.

As soon as they stepped from the pool, they wrapped the boys in snuggly towels. Ryder rubbed Travis's arms. She did the same with Tyler and he smiled at her. Her heart swelled at his sweetness. "You are such a good boy. Isn't he?" she said to Ryder.

"You bet," Ryder said and pressed his mouth against Tyler's chubby cheek, making a buzzing sound. Tyler chortled with joy.

"That sound is magic," she said.

Ryder nodded as he continued to rub Travis. "Yeah, it is." His glance raked her from head to toe and he shook his head. "You look pretty damn good."

Bridget felt a warmth spread from her belly to her chest and face, down her legs, all the way to her toes. "It's just been a long time for you," she said and turned away to put some clothes on Tyler.

A second later, she felt Ryder's bare chest against her back. An immediate visceral response rocked through her and she was torn between jumping out of her skin and melting. "Yeah, it has," he said. "But that shouldn't make you so damn different from every other woman I've met."

Her stomach dipped. "Stop flattering me," she said. "Get your baby dressed. You don't want him chilled."

After pizza and a raucous bath time, Ryder and Bridget rocked the babies and put them to bed. Ryder would have preferred to usher Bridget into his bed and reacquaint himself with the curves he'd glimpsed in the pool, but he would have to bide his time. Hopefully not too long, he told himself as his gaze strayed to the way her hips moved in her cotton skirt. He'd thought he was so smart getting her out of most of her clothes by inviting her to the baby swimming class. Now he would live with those images all night long.

"Wine?" he asked, lifting a bottle from the kitchen before he joined her in the den.

She had sunk onto the sofa and leaned her head back against it, unintentionally giving him yet another seductive photo for his mental collection. One silky leg crossed over the other while the skirt hugged her hips. The V-neck of her black shirt gave him just a glimpse of creamy cleavage. For once, her lips were bare, but that didn't stop him from wanting to kiss her.

Her eyes opened to slight slits shrouded with the dark fan of her eyelashes. "One glass," she said. "I think everyone will sleep well tonight."

Speak for yourself, he thought wryly and poured her wine. He allowed himself one glass because he wasn't on call.

"It's amazing how much they can scream, isn't it?" she said as he sat beside her.

"They save up energy lying around all the time. It's not like they can play football or baseball yet."

"Have you thought about which sport you'll want them to pursue?" she asked.

"Whatever keeps them busy and tired. If they're busy and tired, they won't be as likely to get into trouble," he said.

"So that's the secret," she said with a slow smile. "Did that work for you?"

"Most of the time. I learned at a young age that I wanted a different life than the life my parents had."

"Hmm, at least you knew your parents," she said.

"Can't say knowing my father was one of my strong points."

"Well, you know what they say, if you can't be a good example, be a terrible warning."

He chuckled slightly and relaxed next to her. "I don't want to be the same kind of father he was. Drunk. Neglectful. Bordering on abusive."

"You couldn't be those things," she said.

"Why not? You've heard the saying, an apple doesn't fall too far from the tree."

"You've already fallen a long way from that so-called tree," she said. "Plus, you may be fighting some of your feelings, but you love those boys." She lifted her hand to his jaw. "You have a good heart. I liked that about you from the first time I met you."

"And I thought it was my singing voice," he said and lowered his mouth to hers, reveling in the anticipation he felt inside and saw in her eyes.

She tasted like a delicious combination of red wine, tiramisu and something forbidden that he wasn't going to resist. Ryder was certain he could resist her if he wanted. If there was one thing Ryder possessed, it was self-discipline. The quality had been necessary to get him through med school, residency and even more so now in his position at the hospital and with the twins.

For now, though, Ryder had decided he didn't want to resist Bridget. With her lush breasts pressing against his chest, discipline was the last thing on his mind. She was so voluptuously female from her deceptively airy attitude to her curvy body. He slid one of his hands through her hair as she wiggled against him.

A groan of pleasure and want rose from his throat as she deepened the kiss, drawing his tongue into her mouth. The move echoed what he wanted to be doing with the rest of his body and hers. He wrapped his hands around her waist. He slid one down to her hips and the other upward to just under her breast.

He was so hard that he almost couldn't breathe. She was so soft, so feminine, so hot. With every beat of his heart, he craved her. He wanted to consume her, to slide inside her….

Ryder slid his hand to her breast, cupping its fullness. Her nipple peaked against his palm. The fire inside him rising, he tugged a few buttons of her blouse loose and slipped his hand under her bra, touching her bare skin, which made him want to touch every inch of her. He couldn't remember wanting to inhale a woman before.

The next natural step would be to remove her clothes and his and after that, caress her with his hands and mouth. After that, he wanted to slide inside her…. She would be so hot, so wet….

All he wanted was to be as close to her as humanly possible.

From some peripheral area of his brain, he heard a knock and then another. Her body and soul called to him. He took her mouth in another deep kiss.

Another knock sounded, this time louder, but Ryder was determined to ignore it.

Suddenly his front door opened and Marshall burst into the room.

"Whoa," Marshall said. "Sorry to interrupt."

Ryder felt Bridget pull back and hastily arrange her shirt. "Who—" she said in a breathless voice.

"My best friend from high school, Marshall," Ryder said. "He has a key," he continued in a dark voice.

Marshall lifted his hands. "Hey, I called and you

didn't answer. I started getting worried. You almost always answer at night. We've had a beer three times during the last week." His friend stared at Bridget and gave a low whistle. "And who do we have here?"

Irritated, Ryder scowled. "Show a little respect. Prin—" He stopped when Bridget pinched his arm. Staring at her in disbelief, he could see that she didn't want him to reveal her title. "Bridget Devereaux, this is Marshall Bailey."

His friend moved forward and extended his hand. Bridget stood and accepted the courtesy.

"Nice to meet you, Bridget," Marshall said. "It's a relief to see Ryder with a woman."

Embarrassment slammed through Ryder and he also stood. "Marshall," he said in a warning tone.

"I didn't mean that the way it sounded. The poor guy hasn't had much company except me and the twins." Marshall cleared his throat. "How did you two meet anyway?"

"Okay, enough, Mr. Busybody. As you can see, I'm fine, so you can leave."

"Oh no, that's not necessary," Bridget said and glanced at her watch. "I really should be leaving. I have an early flight tomorrow."

"Where?" Ryder asked.

"Chicago. They have a teaching hospital. I'll be meeting with the hospital chief to present the proposal for Chantaine's medical exchange."

"Oh," he said, surprised at the gut punch of disappointment he felt when he should feel relieved. "I guess this means you've given up on our residents."

"No, but you haven't been at all receptive. My brother

Stefan has instructed me to explore other possibilities. Your program was our first choice due to the quality of your residents and also the fact that you have so many family doctors and prevention specialists. But because you're unwilling to help…"

"For Pete's sake, Ryder, help the woman out," Marshall said and moved forward. "Is there anything I can do?"

Marshall was really getting on Ryder's nerves. "Not unless you have a medical degree and are licensed to practice," Ryder said.

"I believe my driver is here. Thank you for an action-packed evening," she said with a smile full of sexy amusement.

Ryder would have preferred a different kind of action. "I'll walk you to the car," he said, then shot a quick glance at Marshall. "I'll be back in a minute."

Ryder escorted Bridget to the limo waiting at the curb. A man stood ready to open the door for her. Ryder was disappointed as hell that she was headed out of town. Stupid. "So how long will you be gone?" he asked.

She lifted a dark eyebrow and her lips tilted in a teasing grin. "Are you going to miss me, Dr. McCall?"

His gut twisted. "That would be crazy. The only thing I've been missing for the last month is sleep," he lied.

"Oh, well, maybe you'll get lucky and get some extra sleep while I'm gone. Ta-ta," she said and turned toward the limo.

He caught her wrist and drew her back against him. The man at the car door took a step toward them, but she waved her hand. "Not necessary, Raoul."

"You must enjoy tormenting me," he said.

"Me?" she said, her blue eyes wide with innocence. "How could I possibly have the ability to torment you?"

"I don't know, but you sure as hell do," he muttered and kissed her, which only served to make him hotter. He turned her own words on her. "So, Your Highness, what are you going to do about it?"

She gave a sharp intake of breath and her eyes darkened as if her mind were working the same way as his. She bit her lip. "I can call you when I return from Chicago."

"Do that," he said.

Ryder returned to his house to find Marshall lounging on the sofa and drinking a glass of red wine. "This isn't bad," he said.

"Glad you like it. In the future, give me a call before you drop in. Okay?"

Marshall looked injured. "I did call you. You just didn't answer." He shook his head and gave a low whistle. "And now I understand why. That's one hot babe, and she reeks money. A limo came to pick her up? You sure know how to pick 'em. How did you meet her?"

"In an elevator," Ryder said, not wanting to give away too many details. As much as he liked his old friend, Ryder knew Marshall could gossip worse than an old lady.

"Really?" Marshall said, dumbfounded. "An elevator. Was it just you and her? Did you do anything—adventurous?"

"Not the way you're thinking," Ryder said in a dry tone, although if it had been just him and Bridget in that elevator without the twins, his mind would have gone in the same direction.

"Well, I'm glad you're finally getting some action," Marshall said.

Ryder swore. "I'd say you pretty much nixed that tonight. Between you and the twins, who needs birth control?"

Marshall chuckled. "Sorry, bud, better luck next time. I thought I'd see if Suzanne was hanging around tonight. She stays late for you sometimes."

Realization struck Ryder. "You didn't come by to see me. You came to see my nanny. I'm telling you now. Keep your hands off my nanny. She's not your type."

"Who says?"

"I say."

"Why isn't she my type? She's pretty. She's nice," he said.

"She's six years older than you are," Ryder said.

"So? She doesn't look it. She's got a fresh look about her and she's sweet. Got a real nice laugh," Marshall said.

"I'm not liking what I'm hearing," Ryder said, stepping between Marshall and the television. "So far, Suzanne is the perfect nanny. I don't want you messing with her. The boys and I need her."

"She's an adult. She can decide if she wants me to mess with her," he said with a shrug.

"Marshall," he said in a dead-serious voice. "She's not like your dime-a-dozen girls running fast and loose. She's not used to a guy like you who'll get her in the sack and leave her like yesterday's garbage."

Marshall winced. "No need to insult me. I've had a few long-term relationships."

"Name them," Ryder challenged.

"Well, there was that redhead, Wendy. She and I saw each other for at least a couple of years."

"She lived out of town, didn't she?" Ryder asked. "How many other women were you seeing at the same time?"

Marshall scowled. "Okay, what about Sharona? We lived together."

"For how long?"

"Seven weeks, but—"

"Enough said. Keep your paws off Suzanne."

Marshall slugged down the rest of the wine and stood. "You know, I'm not a rotten guy."

"Never said you were."

"I just haven't ever found the right girl," Marshall said.

"As long as you and I understand that Suzanne is not the right girl for you, everything will be fine."

Three days later, Bridget returned from her trip to Chicago. She hadn't snagged any doctors, but she'd persuaded one of the specialists she'd met to visit Chantaine and offer lectures and demonstrations. She was getting closer to her goal. She could feel it. Even though what she really wanted to do tonight was soak in a tub and watch television, she was committed to attend a charity event for Alzheimer's with the governor's son, who was actually quite a bit older than she was. Part of the job, she told herself as she got ready. She thought about calling Ryder, but every time she thought about him, she felt a jumpiness in her stomach. Bridget wasn't sure how far she wanted to go with him because she knew she would be leaving Dallas as soon as she accomplished her mission.

There was something about the combination of his strength and passion that did things to her. It was exciting. And perplexing.

Preferring to have her own chauffeur, Bridget met Robert Goodwin, the governor's son, in the lobby of her hotel. He was a distinguished-looking man in his mid-forties who reminded her of one of her uncles. She decided that was how she would treat him.

Her bodyguard Raoul, who occasionally played double duty in making introductions, stepped forward. "Your Highness, Robert Goodwin."

She nodded and extended her hand. "Lovely to meet you, Mr. Goodwin. Thank you for escorting me to an event that will raise awareness for such an important cause."

"My pleasure, Your Highness," he said, surprising her when he brought her hand to his mouth. "Please call me Robert. May I say that you look breathtaking?"

"Thank you very much, Robert. Shall we go?"

By the time they arrived at the historical hall, Bridget concluded that Mr. Goodwin's intentions were not at all uncle-like and she prepared herself for a sticky evening. Cameras flashed as they exited the limo and Mr. Goodwin appeared to want to linger for every possible photo as he bragged about her title to the reporters.

"Everyone is excited to have a real princess at the event tonight. People paid big bucks to sit at our table."

"I'm delighted I could help the cause." Sometimes it amazed her that a single spermatozoa had determined her status. And that spermatozoa had originated from a cheating jerk of a man who had never gotten her first name right. Her father.

"Would you join me in a dance?" Robert said, his gaze dipping to her cleavage.

"Thank you, but I need to powder my nose," she said. "Can you tell me where the ladies' room is?"

Robert blinked. "I believe it's down the hall to the left."

"Excuse me," she said and headed for the restroom, fully aware that Raoul was watching. She wondered if she could plead illness. After stalling for several moments, she left and slowly walked toward her table. Halfway there, Ryder stepped in front of her.

"Busy as ever," he said.

Her heart raced at the sight of him. "So true. I arrived back in town this afternoon and had to turn right around to get ready for this event."

"With the governor's son," Ryder said, clearly displeased.

"He could be my uncle," she said.

"Bet that's not what he's thinking," Ryder countered.

She grimaced and shrugged. "It's not the first time I've had to manage unwelcome interest, and if my appearance generates additional income for this good cause…"

"True," he said, his eyes holding a misery that grabbed at her.

"What brings you here?"

"Dr. Walters. He has had an impact on hundreds of doctors, but now he can't recognize himself in the mirror."

"I'm so sorry," she said, her heart hurting at the

expression on his face. "Seeing you, hearing you, makes me glad I came. I'm ashamed to confess that I was tempted to cancel because I was so tired after returning from Chicago."

His gaze held hers for a long emotional moment. "I'm glad you didn't give in to your weariness this time."

"Even though I have to face Mr. Anything-but-Good Robert Goodwin," she said.

"Give me a sign and I'll have your back," he said.

She took a deep breath. "That's good to know. I can usually handle things. This isn't the first time."

His gaze swept over her from head to toe and back again. "That's no surprise."

Her stomach dipped and she cleared her throat. "I should get back to my table. I'm told people paid to sit with me. I'm sure it has nothing to do with my title."

His lips twitched. "Not if they really knew you," he said.

"You flatter me," she said.

"Not because you're a princess," he said.

"Call me tomorrow."

"I will," he said.

Bridget returned to her table and tried to be her most charming self and at the same time not encouraging Robert Goodwin. It was challenging, but she was determined.

After the meal had been served, he turned to her. "I'm determined to dance with you."

"I'm not that good of a dancer," she assured him.

He laughed, his gaze dipping over her cleavage again. "I'm a good leader," he said and rose, extending his hand to her. "Let me surprise you."

Or not, she thought wishing with all her heart that he wouldn't surprise her. She didn't want to embarrass the man. She lifted her lips in a careful smile. "One dance," she said and stood.

They danced to a waltz, but he somehow managed to rub against her. She tried to back away, but he wrapped his hands around her waist like a vise, drawing him against her. Suddenly, she saw Ryder behind Robert Goodwin, his hand on his shoulder. Robert appeared surprised.

"Can I cut in?" Ryder asked.

Robert frowned. "I'm not—"

"Yes," Bridget said. "It's only proper."

Robert reluctantly released her and Ryder swept her into his arms.

"Thank goodness," she murmured.

He wrapped his arms around her and it felt entirely different than it had with Robert. She stared into his eyes and felt a shockwave roll through her. "When did you learn to dance?"

"A generous woman taught me during medical school," he said, drawing her closer, yet not too close.

Bridget felt a spike of envy but forced it aside. "She did an excellent job."

He chuckled. "It was all preparation," he said. "Everything we do is preparation for what waits for us in the future."

"I would have to be quite arrogant to think your preparation was for me," she said, feeling light-headed.

"You look beautiful tonight," he said, clearly changing the subject. "I hate having to share you with anyone else."

Her stomach dipped. "It's part of who I was born to be. Duty calls," she said.

"But what does Bridget want?" he challenged. "Meet me in the foyer in fifteen minutes."

"How?" she asked.

"You'll figure it out," he said.

Chapter Five

She would figure it out, Bridget thought as she surreptitiously glanced at the diamond-encrusted watch that had belonged to her grandmother. Two minutes to go and she was supposed to be introduced to the crowd within the next moment.

"As we continue to introduce our honored guests, we'd like to present Her Highness, Princess Bridget Devereaux of the country of Chantaine."

Bridget stood and smiled and waved to the applauding crowd. She hadn't known she was a table head, but it wasn't unusual for event organizers to put her in the spotlight given the chance. Because of her title, she was a source of curiosity and interest.

Spotting Ryder leaning against the back wall as he pointed to his watch, she quickly squeezed her hand together and flashed her five fingers, indicating she needed more time. Then she sank into her seat.

Robert leaned toward her. "I was cheated out of my dance. We need to hit the floor again."

"I wish I could, but my ankle is hurting," she said.

Robert scowled. "Maybe because of the man who cut in on our dance."

She lifted her shoulders. "Perhaps it's the long day catching up with me."

"You're too generous. We could try a slow dance," he said in a low voice.

"Oh no, I couldn't hurt your feet that way," she said. "But I would like to freshen up. Please excuse me," she said and rose, wondering why she was going to such extremes to meet Ryder when she was supposed to be concentrating on making an appearance.

Her heart was slamming against her rib cage as she tried to take a sideways route through the tables along the perimeter of the room. With every step, part of her chanted *This is crazy—this is crazy.* But she kept on walking, so she must indeed be crazy. She stepped into the foyer and glanced around the area.

Something snagged her hand. She glanced over her shoulder and spotted Ryder as he pulled her with him down a hallway. "Where are we—"

"Trust me," he said and pulled her toward the first door they came upon. It was an empty dark room with a stack of chairs pushed against a wall.

"What are we doing?" she asked, breathlessly clinging to him.

"Hell if I know," he said, sliding his hands through her hair and tilting her head toward his. "I feel like a car with no brakes headed straight for you."

"So, we're both crazy," she said.

"Looks that way," he said and lowered his mouth to hers.

Her knees turned to water and she clung to him. His strength made her feel alive despite how tired she felt from her long day of travel. Shocked at his effect on her, she loved the sensation of his hard chest against her breasts. She wanted to feel his naked skin against hers. She growled, unable to get close enough.

He swore under his breath as his hands roamed over her waist and up to the sides of her breasts. "I can't get enough of you," he muttered and took her mouth in a deep kiss again.

She felt dizzy with a want and need she denied on a regular basis. It was as if she was suffering from a more delicious version of altitude sickness. His mouth against hers made her hotter with every stroke of his tongue. More than anything, she wanted to feel him against her.

"Ryder," she whispered, tugging at his tie and dropping her mouth to his neck.

He gave a groan of arousal. "Come home with me. Now," he said, squeezing her derriere with one hand and clasping her breast with the other.

Too tempted for words, she felt the tug and pull of duty and courtesy over her own needs. Bloody hell, why couldn't she just this once be selfish, irresponsible and rude? A sound of complete frustration bubbled from her throat. Because she just couldn't. She was in the States on official business from Chantaine and she'd been assigned to represent a cause important to her and her people.

"I can't," she finally managed. "It would just be

wrong and rude and it's not just about me. I'm sorry," she whispered.

"I don't know what it is about you, but you make me want to be more reckless than I've ever been in my life. More reckless than flying down Deadman's Hill on my bicycle with no hands when I was ten."

Bridget felt the same way, but she was holding on by the barest thread of self-restraint. Suddenly the door whooshed open and closed, sending her heart into her throat. Her head cleared enough to realize this situation could provide the press with an opportunity to paint her family in a bad light.

She held her breath, waiting for a voice, but none sounded.

"It's okay," he said as if he understood without her saying a word. "Whoever opened the door must have glanced inside and not spotted us. I'll leave first, then you wait a minute or two before you leave. I'll warn you if it looks like there's a crowd waiting for you."

She paused, then nodded slowly.

Ryder gave her shoulders a reassuring squeeze and kissed her quickly, then walked toward the door. Bridget stood frozen to the floor for several breaths and gave herself a quick shake. She moved to the door and listened, but the door was too thick. She couldn't hear anything. Counting to a hundred, she cracked open the door and peeked outside. No crowd. No photogs. Relief coursed through her and she stepped outside.

"Your Highness, I was worried about you," Robert said from behind her.

Her stomach muscles tightened and she quickly turned. "Robert, how kind of you."

"What were you doing in there?" he asked.

"My sense of direction is dismal," she said. "I went right when I should have turned left. Thank you for coming to my rescue. Now I can return to our table."

He slid his hand behind her waist and she automatically stiffened, but he seemed to ignore her response. "We can leave, if you like. I could take you to my condo...."

"Again, you're being kind, but we're here for an important cause."

"Afterward—"

"It's been a full day for me flying from Chicago. I appreciate your understanding that I'll be desperate to finally retire," she said. One of her advisers had instructed her that one should speak to another person as if they possessed good qualities...even if they didn't.

"Another time, then," Robert said, clearly disappointed.

Bridget gave a noncommittal smile, careful not to offer any false hope.

When Bridget didn't hear from Ryder for three days, she began to get peeved. Actually, she was peeved after day one. He'd behaved like he was starving for her and couldn't wait another moment, then didn't call. She considered calling him at least a dozen times, but her busy schedule aided her in her restraint.

On Tuesday, however, she was scheduled to meet with a preventative adult health specialist in preparation for a video she would be filming with the doctor as a public service announcement for Chantaine.

Afterward, she meandered down the hall past his

office. She noticed Ryder wasn't there, but his assistant was. Bridget gave in to temptation and stepped into the office. "Hello. I was wondering if Dr. McCall is in today."

The assistant sighed. "Dr. McCall is making rounds and seeing interns, but he may need to leave early for family reasons. May I take a message?"

"Not necessary," she demurred, but wondered what those family reasons were. "Are the twins okay?" she couldn't help asking.

The assistant nodded. "I think so. It's the nanny—" The phone rang. "Excuse me."

The nanny! The nanny she'd selected for Ryder and the boys had been as perfect as humanly possible. Perhaps more perfect. What could have possibly happened? Resisting the urge to grill the assistant about her, she forced herself to walk away. Her fingers itched to call him, but she didn't. It would be rude to interrupt his appointments with patients or the residents.

Bothered, bothered, bothered, she stalked through the hallway. The pediatric department head saw her and stopped in front of her, smiling. "Your Highness, what a pleasure to see you."

"Thank you, Doctor. How are you?" she said more than asked.

"Great. Would you like to get together for dinner?" he asked.

"I would, but I must confess my immediate schedule is quite demanding. Perhaps some other time," she said.

"I'll keep asking," he said and gave her a charming smile that didn't move her one iota.

Brooding, she walked down the hall and out of the hospital to the limo that awaited her. A text would be less intrusive, she decided, and sent a message. Two minutes later, she received a response. *Nanny had emergency appendectomy. Juggling with backup.*

WHY DIDN'T YOU CALL ME? she texted in return.

Her phone rang one moment later and she answered. "Hello."

"It's been crazy. I've even had to ask Marshall for help."

"Why didn't you ask me?" she demanded.

"You told me your schedule was picking up. I figured you wouldn't have time," he said.

True, she thought, but she was still bothered. "You still should have called me."

"You're a busy princess. What could you have done?" he asked.

Good question. She closed her eyes. "I could have rearranged my schedule so I could help you."

Silence followed. "You would do that?"

She bit her lip. "Yes."

"I didn't think of that."

"Clearly," she said.

He chuckled. "In that case, can you come over tomorrow afternoon? My part-time nanny needs a break."

"I'll confirm by five o'clock tonight," she said. "I have to make a few calls."

"Impressive," he said. "I bet your reschedules are going to be disappointed. Too bad," he said without a trace of sympathy.

She laughed. "I'll call you later," she said and they hung up and her heart felt ten times lighter.

The following afternoon, Bridget relieved the backup nanny while the twins were sleeping. From previous experience, she knew her moments of silence were numbered. She used the time to prepare bottles and snacks for the boys.

Sure enough, the first cry sounded. She raced upstairs and opened the door. Travis was sitting up in his crib wearing a frowny face.

"Hello, sweet boy," she whispered.

He paused mid-wail and stared at her wide-eyed.

"Hi," she whispered and smiled.

Travis smiled and lifted his fingers to his mouth.

Bridget changed his diaper. Seconds later, Tyler awakened and began to babble. Tyler was the happier baby. He was a bit more fearful, but when he woke up, he didn't start crying immediately.

Bridget wound Travis's mobile and turned her attention to Tyler. She took each baby downstairs ready to put them in their high chairs. Snacks, bottles, books, Baby Einstein and finally Ryder arrived carrying a bottle of wine.

"How's everybody?" he asked, his gaze skimming over her and the boys, then back to her. "Did they wear you out?"

"Not too much yet," she said. "It helps to have a plan."

He nodded. "With alternatives. I ordered Italian, not pizza. It should be delivered soon."

"Thank you," she said.

"I'm hoping to lure you into staying the night," he said.

"Ha, ha," she said. "The trouble with luring me after an afternoon with the twins is that I'll be comatose by nine o'clock at the latest. I talked to your part-time sitter and she told me Suzanne will be out for a few more days. Is that true?"

He nodded. "She had laparoscopic surgery, so her recovery should be much easier than if she'd had an open appendectomy."

"Then I think the next step is to get a list of your backup sitters and inform them of the situation and make a schedule for the children's care. So if you don't mind giving me your names and contact information, I can try to get it straight tomorrow."

He blinked at her in amazement. "You're deceptively incredible," he said. "You give this impression of being lighthearted and maybe a little superficial. Then you turn around and volunteer to take care of my boys, recruit doctors for your country and make countless appearances."

"Oooh, I like that. Deceptively incredible," she said, a bit embarrassed by his flattery. "Many of us are underestimated. It can be a hindrance and a benefit. I try to find the benefit."

Ryder leaned toward her, studying her face. "Have you always been underestimated?"

She considered his question for a moment, then nodded. "I think so. I'm number four out of six and female, so I think I got lost in the mix. I'm not sure my father ever really knew my name, and my mother was beginning to realize that her marriage to my father was not going to be a fairy tale."

"Why not?"

"You must swear to never repeat this," she said.

"I swear, although I'm not sure anyone I know would be interested," he said.

"True enough," she said. "My father was a total philanderer. Heaven knows, my mother tried. I mean, six children? She was a true soldier, though, and gave him two sons. Bless her."

"So what do you want for yourself?" he asked. "You don't want the kind of marriage your parents had."

"Who would?" she said and took a deep breath. "I haven't thought a lot about it. Whenever Stefan has brought up the idea of my marrying someone, I just start laughing and don't stop. Infuriates the blazes out of him," she said, and smiled.

"You didn't answer my question," he said.

His eyes felt as if they bored a hole through her brain, and Bridget realized one of the reasons she was drawn to Ryder was because she couldn't fool him. It was both a source of frustration and relief.

"I'm still figuring it out. For a long time, I've enjoyed the notion of being the eccentric princess who lives in Italy most of the year and always has an Italian boyfriend as her escort."

"Italian boyfriend," he echoed, clearly not pleased.

"You have to agree, it's the antithesis of my current life."

"And I suspect this life wouldn't include children," he continued with a frown.

Feeling defensive, she bit her lip. "Admit it. The life

you'd planned didn't include children…at least for a long while, did it?"

He hesitated.

"Be honest. I was," she said.

"No," he finally admitted. "But not because I was in Italy with an Italian girlfriend."

"No, you were planning to do something more important. A career in medicine. Perfectly noble and worthy, but it would be hard to make a child a priority when you have the kind of passion you do for your career. A child would be…inconvenient."

He took a deep breath. "We choose our careers for many reasons. I wanted to feel like I had the power to help, to cure, to make a difference. It was more important for me to feel as if I were accomplishing those goals than building a family life." He shrugged. "My family life sucked."

"There you go," she said in complete agreement. "My family life sucked, too. In fact, I wanted to get so far away from it that I wanted to move to a different country."

He chuckled. "So how is it that Princess Bridget is changing diapers and taking care of my twins?"

Bridget resisted the urge to squirm. "I won't lie. I once thought children were a lot of trouble and not for me, but then I got a couple of adorable nieces. I still thought I wouldn't want to deal with them for more than a couple hours at most with the nanny at hand to change diapers, of course." She bit her lip. "But it's just so different when they're looking at you with those big eyes, helpless and needing you…. And it would just feel so terribly wrong not to take care of them."

"And how do I fit into it?" he asked, dipping his head toward her.

"You are just an annoying distraction," she said in a mockingly dismissive whisper.

"Well, at least I'm distracting," he said and lowered his mouth to hers.

Bridget felt herself melt into the leather upholstery. She inhaled his masculine scent and went dizzy with want. He was the one thing she'd never had but always wanted and couldn't get enough of. How could that be? She'd been exposed to everything and every kind of person, hadn't she?

But Ryder was different.

She drew his tongue deeper into her mouth and slid her arms around his neck. Unable to stop herself, she wiggled against him and moaned. He groaned in approval, which jacked her up even more.

From some corner of her mind, she heard a sound.

"Eh."

Pushing it aside, she continued to kiss Ryder.

"Eh."

Bridget frowned, wondering….

"Wahhhhhhh."

She reluctantly tore her mouth from Ryder's. "The babies," she murmured breathlessly, glancing down at Travis as he tuned up. The baby had fallen on his side and he couldn't get back up.

"Yeah, I know," Ryder said. "I'm starting to understand the concept of unrequited l—"

"Longing," she finished for him because she couldn't deal with Ryder saying the four-letter L word. It wasn't possible.

"Bet there's a dirty diaper involved," Ryder muttered as he tilted Travis upright.

"Could be," she said and couldn't bring herself to offer to change it. She covered her laugh by clearing her throat. "I wouldn't want to deprive you of your fatherly duty."

He gave her a slow, sexy grin. "I'll just bet you wouldn't."

"It's an important bonding activity," she said, trying to remain serious, but a giggle escaped.

"Can't hold it against you too much," he said. "You've been here all afternoon."

Bridget rose to try to collect herself. Her emotions were all over the place. Walking to the downstairs powder room, she closed the door behind her and splashed water against her cheeks and throat. Sanity, she desperately needed sanity.

The doorbell rang and she returned as Ryder tossed the diaper into the trash before he answered the door. He paid the delivery man and turned around, and Bridget felt her heart dip once, twice, three times…. Adrenaline rushed through her, and she tried to remember a charming, gorgeous Italian man who had affected her this way. When had any man affected her this way?

Oh, heavens, she needed to get away from him. She felt like that superhero. What was his name? Superman. And Ryder was that substance guaranteed to weaken him. What was it? Started with a K…

"Smells good. Hope you like lasagna," Ryder said.

"I can't stay," she said.

"What?" he asked, his brow furrowing.

"I can't stay. I have work to do," she said.

"What work?" he asked.

"Rescheduling my meetings and appearances. I also need to take care of the childcare arrangements for the twins."

He walked slowly toward her, his gaze holding hers. She felt her stomach tumble with each of his steps. "You're not leaving because you have work to do, are you?"

She lifted her chin. "I'm a royal. I always have work to do."

He cupped her chin with his hand. "But the reason you're leaving is not because of work, is it?"

Her breath hitched in her throat.

"You're a chicken, aren't you?" he said. "Princess Cluck Cluck."

"That was rude," she said.

"Cluck, cluck," he said and pressed his mouth against hers.

After making the schedule for the twins' care, Bridget paid her sister an overdue visit. Valentina had threatened to personally drag her away from Dallas if Bridget didn't come to the ranch. Her sister burst down the steps to the porch as Bridget's limo pulled into the drive.

"Thank goodness you're finally here," Tina said.

Bridget laughed as she embraced her sister. "You act like I've been gone for years."

"I thought you would be spending far more time here, but you've been appearing at events, traveling to Chicago. And what's this about you helping that physician with his twin babies? Haven't you helped him enough?"

"It's complicated," Bridget said. "He's had some childcare issues. I think they're mostly resolved now."

"Well, good. I think you've helped him quite enough. Now you can spend some time with me," Tina said as she led Bridget into the house. "I have wonderful plans for us. Two aestheticians are coming to the ranch tomorrow to give massages and facials then we spend the afternoon at the lake."

"Lake?" Bridget echoed. All she'd seen was dry land.

"It's wonderful," Tina reassured her. "The summer heat and humidity can get unbearable here. We have a pond with a swing, but we're going to the lake because Zach got a new boat. Zach and one of his friends will be joining us tomorrow afternoon. Then we'll have baby back ribs for dinner."

Bridget's antennae went up at the mention of Zach's friend. "You're not trying to set me up, are you?"

"Of course not. I just thought you'd enjoy some no-pressure male companionship. Troy is just a nice guy. He also happens to be good-looking and eligible. And if you two should hit it off, then you could live close to me and—" Tina paused and a guilty expression crossed her face. "Okay, it's a little bit of a setup. But not too much," she said quickly. "Troy and Zach are business associates, so we'll have to drag them away from talk about the economy."

Bridget's mind automatically turned to Ryder. There was no reason for her to feel even vaguely committed to him. Her stomach tightened. What did that mean? she wondered. "I'm not really looking right now," Bridget said.

"I know," Tina said. "As soon as you take care of the

doctor project, you're off to Italy and part of that will include flirtations with any Italian man who grabs your fancy. But if someone here grabs your fancy…"

"Tina," Bridget said in a warning voice.

"I hear you," Tina said. "Let's focus on your amazing niece."

"Sounds good to me. I've missed the little sweetheart," Bridget said as they walked into the kitchen.

"Missed her, but not me!" Tina said.

Bridget laughed. "I adore you. Why are you giving me such a hard time?"

Tina lifted her hand to Bridget's face and looked deep into her gaze. "I don't know. I worry about you. I wonder what's going on inside you. You smile, you laugh, but there's a darkness in your eyes."

Bridget's heart dipped at her sister's sensitivity, then she deadpanned. "Maybe it's my new eyeliner."

Tina rolled her eyes. "You're insufferable. I always said that about Stefan, but you're the same, just in a different way."

"I believe I've just been insulted," Bridget said.

"You'll get over it. Hildie made margaritas for us and she always makes doubles."

Chapter Six

Bridget's morning massage coupled with one of Hildie's margaritas had turned her bones to butter. By the time she joined Tina, Zach and Troy on the boat, she was so relaxed that she could have gone to sleep for a good two hours. For politeness' sake, she tried to stay awake, although she kept her dark sunglasses firmly in place to hide her drooping eyelids.

Troy Palmer was a lovely Texas gentleman, a bit bulkier than Ryder. Of course Ryder was so busy he rarely took time to eat. A server offered shrimp and lobster while they lounged on the boat.

"Nice ride," Troy said to Zach.

Zach smiled as Tina leaned against his chest. "My wife thought I was crazy. She said I would be too busy."

"Time will tell," Tina said. "But if this makes you take a few more breaks, then I'm happy."

"You're not neglecting my sister, are you?" Bridget asked as she sipped a bottle of icy cold water.

Zach lifted a dark eyebrow. "There's a fine line between being the companion and keeper of a princess."

"I believe that's what you Americans call baloney. You work because you must. It's the kind of man you are. I love you for it," Tina said. "But I also love the time we have together."

Zach's face softened. "I love you, too, sweetheart."

Bridget cleared her throat. "We're delighted that you love each other," Bridget said. "But I'm going to have to dive overboard if we don't change the subject."

Tina giggled. "As you wish. Troy, tell us about your latest trip to Italy."

"Italy?" Bridget echoed.

"I thought that might perk you up," Tina said.

Troy shrugged his shoulders. "I go three or four times a year. Business, but I usually try to work in a trip to Florence."

"Oh, Florence," Bridget said longingly. "One of my favorite places in the world."

Troy nodded. "Yeah, I also like to slip down to Capri every now and then…"

Bridget's cell phone vibrated in the pocket of her cover-up draped over the side of her chair. She tried to ignore it, but wondered if Ryder was calling her. Dividing her attention between Troy's discussion about Italy and thoughts of Ryder, she nodded even though she wasn't hanging onto his every word. Her phone vibrated again and she was finding it difficult to concentrate.

She grabbed her cover-up and stood. "Please excuse me. I need to powder my nose."

"To the right and downstairs," Zach said. "And it's small," he warned.

"No problem," she said cheerfully and walked around the corner. She lifted her phone to listen to her messages. As she listened, her heart sank. Tomorrow's sitter was canceling. She was calling Bridget because Ryder was in surgery and unreachable.

Pacing at the other end of the boat, she tried the other backup sitters and came up empty. Reluctantly, she called Marshall who answered immediately.

"Marshall," he said. "'Sup?"

"Hello, Marshall," she said. "This is Bridget Devereaux."

"The princess," he said. Ryder had told her that Marshall had performed a web search and learned who she was. "Princess calling me. That's cool."

"Yes," she said, moving toward the other end of the boat. "There's some difficulty with sitting arrangements for Ryder's boys tomorrow morning. I was hoping you could help me with a solution."

"Tomorrow morning," he said. "Whoa, that's a busy day for me."

"Yes, I'm so sorry. I would normally try to fill in, but I'm out of town at the moment," she said.

"I might have a friend—"

"No," she said. "As you know, Ryder is very particular about his backup sitters. He won't leave the twins with just anyone."

"True," Marshall said. "Although I'm last on the list."

Silence followed.

"I'm last on the list, aren't I?" Marshall asked.

"Well, you're an entrepreneur," she managed. "Ryder

knows you're a busy man with many demands on your time."

"Yeah," Marshall said. "How much time does he need?"

"Five hours," she said, wincing as she said it.

Marshall whistled. "That's gonna be tough."

"Let me see what I can do," she said. "I'll make some more calls."

"If you can have someone cover things in the early morning, I could probably come in around ten."

"Thank you so much. I'll do my very best," she said.

"Bridget," Tina said from behind her.

"Bloody hell," she muttered.

Marshall chuckled.

"To whom are you speaking?" Tina demanded.

"A friend," Bridget said. "Forgive me, Marshall. My sister is after me."

"Good luck. Keep me posted," he said.

"Yes, I will," she said and clicked off the phone. She turned to face her sister with a smile. "I'm just working out the timing of an appearance."

"Which appearance is that?" Tina asked.

"In Dallas," Bridget said. "I must say I do love Zach's new toy. I think it will be a fabulous way for the two of you to relax."

"Exactly which appearance in Dallas?" Tina said, studying her with narrowed eyes.

"Stop being so nosy," Bridget said.

Tina narrowed her eyes further. "This is about that doctor with the twins, isn't it?"

"His sitter for tomorrow has cancelled so we have to find another."

"We?"

Bridget sighed. "If you met him, you'd understand. He performs surgery, advises residents and he's an instant father."

"Perhaps he should take some time off to be with his new children," Tina muttered.

"It's not that easy. His mentor has Alzheimer's and he's trying to fill his position unofficially."

Tina studied her. "You're not falling for him, are you?"

Bridget gave a hearty laugh at the same time she fought the terror in her soul. "Of course not. You know I prefer Italian men."

Tina paused, then nodded. "True, and although you love your nieces, you've always said you couldn't imagine having children before you were thirty."

"Exactly," she said, though she felt a strange twinge.

"Hmm," Tina said, still studying her. "Is this doctor good-looking?"

Bridget shrugged. Yes, Ryder was very good-looking, but that wasn't why she found him so compelling. Giving herself a mental eye roll, she knew Tina wouldn't understand. "He's fine," she said. "But he's not Italian."

Tina giggled and put her arm around Bridget. "Now that's our Bridget. That's the kind of answer I would expect from you. Come back and relax with us."

Bridget smiled, but part of her felt uncomfortable. She knew what Tina was saying, that Bridget wasn't a particularly deep person. The truth was she'd never wanted to be deep. If she thought too deeply, she suspected she could become depressed. After all, she'd been a fairly average child, not at all spectacular. She hadn't flunked out in school, but she hadn't excelled at anything either. Except at being cheerful. Or pretending to be cheerful.

"I'll be there in just a moment. I need to make a few calls first."

"Very well, but don't take too long. Troy may not be Italian, but he's very good-looking and spends a fair amount of time in Italy."

"Excellent point," Bridget said, although she felt not the faintest flicker of interest in the man. "I'll be there shortly."

Several moments later, Bridget used all her charm to get the part-time sitter to fill in for the morning. Relieved, she called Marshall to inform him of the change.

"Hey, did you hear from Ryder?" he asked before she could get a word in edgewise.

"No. Should I have?" she asked, confused. "I thought he was in surgery."

"He's apparently out. He just called to tell me Dr. Walters passed away this morning," Marshall said.

Bridget's heart sank. "Oh no."

"Yeah. He's taking it hard. He hadn't seen Dr. Walters in a while and he'd been planning to try to visit him later this week." Marshall sighed. "Dr. Walters was the closest thing to a father Ryder had."

Bridget felt so helpless. "Is there something I can do?"

"Not really," Marshall said. "The twins will keep him busy tonight and that's for the best. The next few days are gonna be tough, though."

She saw her sister walking toward her and felt conflicted. "Thank you for telling me."

"No problem. Thanks for taking care of the childcare for tomorrow morning. Bye for now."

"Goodbye," she said, but he had already disconnected.

"You look upset," Tina said.

"I am."

After 9:30 p.m., Ryder prowled his den with a heavy heart. His mentor was gone. Although Dr. Walters had been mentally gone for a while now, the finality of the man's physical death hit Ryder harder than he'd expected. Maybe it was because he'd lost his brother so recently, too.

Ryder felt completely and totally alone. Sure, he had the twins and his profession, but two of the most important people in the world to him were gone and never coming back. He wondered what it meant that aside from his longtime friend Marshall, he had no other meaningful relationships. Was he such a workaholic that he'd totally isolated himself?

A knock sounded on his door, surprising him. Probably Marshall, he thought and opened the door. To Bridget. His heart turned over.

"Hi," she said, her gaze searching his. She bit her lip. "I know it's late and I don't want to impose—"

He snagged her arm and pulled her inside. "How did you know?"

"Marshall," she said, then shot him a chiding glance. "I would have preferred to hear it from you."

"I thought about it," he said, raking his hand through his hair. "But you've done enough helping with the babies."

"I thought perhaps that you and I were about more

than the babies, but maybe I was wrong," she said, looking away.

His heart slamming against his rib cage, he cupped her chin and swiveled it toward him. "You were right. You know you were."

"Is it just sex? Are you just totally deprived?" she asked in an earnest voice.

He swallowed a chuckle. "I wish."

Her eyes darkened with emotion and she stepped closer. She moved against him and slid her arms upward around the back of his neck. She pulled his face toward hers and he couldn't remember feeling this alive. Ever.

His lips brushed hers and he tried to hold on to his self-control, but it was tough. She slid her moist lips from side to side and he couldn't stand it any longer. He devoured her with his mouth, tasting her, taking her. Seconds later, he realized he might not ever get enough, but damn, he would give it his best shot.

He slid his fingers through her hair and slid his tongue deeper into her mouth. She suckled it and wriggled against him. Her response made him so hard that he wasn't sure he could stand it. His body was on full tilt in the arousal zone.

He took a quick breath and forced himself to draw back. "I'm not sure I can pull back after this," he said, sliding his hands down over her waist and hips. "If you're going to say no, do it now."

Silence hung between them for heart-stopping seconds.

He sucked in another breath. "Bridget—"

"Yes," she whispered. "Yes."

Everything in front of him turned black and white

at the same time. He drew her against him and ran his hands up to her breasts and her hair, then back down again. He wanted to touch every inch of her.

She felt like oxygen to him, like life after he'd been in a tomb. He couldn't get enough of her. He savored the taste and feel of her. Tugging at her blouse, he pushed it aside and slid his hands over her shoulders and lower to the tops of her breasts.

She gave a soft gasp that twisted his gut.

"Okay?" he asked, dipping his thumbs over her nipples.

She gasped again. "Yesssss."

He unfastened her bra and filled his hands with her breasts.

Ryder groaned. Bridget moaned.

"So sexy," he muttered.

She pulled at his shirt and seconds later, her breasts brushed his chest. Ryder groaned again.

The fire inside him exploded and he pushed aside the rest of her clothes and his. He tasted her breasts and slid his mouth lower to her belly and lower still, drawing more gasps and moans from her delicious mouth. Then he thought about contraception. Swearing under his breath, he pulled back for a second. "Give me a few seconds," he said. "You'll thank me later."

He raced upstairs to grab condoms and returned downstairs.

"What?" she asked.

"Trust me," he said and took her mouth again. He slid his hand between her legs and found her wet and wanting.

Unable to hold back one moment longer, he pushed

her legs apart and sank inside her. Bridget clung to him as he pumped inside her. She arched against him, drawing him deep.

He tried to hold out, but she felt so good. Plunging inside her one last time, he felt his climax roar through him. Alive, he felt more alive than he'd felt for as long as he could remember…. "Bridget," he muttered.

Her breath mingled with his and he could sense that she hadn't gone over the top. He was determined to take her there. Sliding his hand between them, he found her sweet spot and began to stroke.

Her breath hitched. The sound was gratifying and arousing. A couple moments later, she stiffened beneath him. He began to thrust again and she came in fits and starts, sending him over the edge.

He couldn't believe his response to her. Twice in such a short time? He wasn't an eighteen-year-old. "Come to bed with me."

"Yes," she said. "If I can make my legs move enough to walk upstairs."

He chuckled and knew the sound was rough. Everything about him felt sated, yet aroused and rough. "I'll help."

"Thank goodness," she said.

He helped her to her feet, but when they arrived at the bottom of the steps, he swept her into his arms and carried her up the stairs.

"Oh, help," she said. "I hope I don't give you a hernia."

"If you do, it'll be worth it," he said.

She swatted at him. "You're supposed to say I'm as light as a feather even though I may weigh half a ton."

"You took the words out of my mouth. You're light as a feather," he said.

She met his gaze and her eyes lit with a glow that both warmed and frightened him. "Excellent response," she said and took his mouth in a sensual kiss that made him dizzy.

"Whoa," he said and stumbled the rest of the way to his room. He set her on the mattress and followed her down. "You smell amazing," he said inhaling her scent. "You taste incredible," he said and dragged his tongue over her throat. "I want to be inside you all night long."

Her breath hitched again and she swung her legs around his hips. Sliding her fingers into his hair, she pulled his mouth to hers. "Do your best," she whispered and he thrust inside her.

Later that night, Bridget awakened, finding herself curled around Ryder. She was clinging to him. Her body said she wanted all of him, as much as he could give, as much as she could receive. But it wasn't just her body that craved him; some part deep inside her felt as if she belonged exactly where she was.

Her breath abandoned her. How was she supposed to manage this, this physical, yet highly emotional relationship with a man like Ryder? It wasn't even a man like Ryder. It was Ryder himself.

Ryder slid his thigh between hers, sending her sensual awareness of him into high mode. "You're awake," he said, sliding his arms around her. "You weren't planning on going anywhere, were you?"

"No. Just thinking."

"I'll put a stop to that," he said and distracted her again with his lovemaking. Afterward, she fell asleep.

The sound of a baby crying awakened her minutes later.... *Had it really been hours?* she wondered as she glanced at the alarm clock. Looking beside her, she saw that Ryder had already left the bed. The second baby started crying and she rose from the bed and pulled on one of Ryder's shirts. Thank goodness it covered her nearly to her knees because she'd left her own clothes downstairs.

She met Ryder in the hallway as he carried a baby in each arm. "Sorry our good-morning song woke you," he said with a wry, sleepy grin. His hair was sleep-mussed and a whisker shadow darkened his chin. Shirtless, he wore a pair of pajama pants that dipped below his belly button. She couldn't remember when he'd looked more sexy.

Reining in her thoughts, she extended her hands to take one of the twins. "I can help."

Tyler immediately fell toward her and she caught him in her arms.

"He made that decision pretty quickly. Can't fault his judgment," he said with a chuckle. "I already changed their diapers."

"Really?" she said, astonished.

"Don't look so surprised," he said as he led the way down the stairs. "My baby-care skills are improving."

"Congratulations," she said and put Tyler into one of the high chairs while Ryder slid Travis into the other high chair. She immediately put a few Cheerios on the trays while she prepared the bottles.

Ryder prepared the oatmeal. "You're getting faster at this baby stuff, too."

"I watched Suzanne one morning and took notes. She's so efficient."

"I'll be glad when she can come back," he said.

"Oh, speaking of that," she said. "The part-time sitter should be here any—"

A knock sounded at the door and Bridget felt a sliver of panic as she glanced at her bare legs and thought of her clothing strewn across the den. "Oh, bloody—Stefan will have my head. I'll be back in a couple moments," she said and grabbed her clothes and scrambled upstairs to get dressed. She glanced in the mirror and tried to tame her hair before she returned to the stairs.

Ryder met her halfway with an inscrutable expression in his eyes. "Embarrassed to be caught with an American doctor?"

"Not embarrassed so much as I wouldn't want my brother Stefan to find out. He really prefers we maintain a squeaky-clean image. And unfortunately we never know when someone may leak something to the press. That can turn into a huge mess."

"So you keep all your lovers hidden?" he asked.

"There haven't been that many," she said. "Do you really want paparazzi standing outside your door assaulting you with questions about me?"

"Good point," he said. "I'm going up to my study for a while. Dr. Walters's wife has asked me to write a eulogy for his memorial service."

Bridget's heart twisted at the grief Ryder was clearly trying to conceal. "I'm so sorry. Are you sure I can't do anything for you?"

His lips twitched. "You did a damn good job distracting me last night."

She felt her cheeks heat. "I was thinking of a cup of tea."

He shook his head. "I drink coffee. Breakfast would be nice, though."

She blinked. "Food. You want me to prepare food?" she echoed, at a loss. She'd taken one cooking class in her younger years and couldn't remember anything from it except how to put out a fire on a stove top.

He chuckled. "Sorry. I forgot your position, Your Highness."

She immediately felt challenged by his tone. "Well, it's not as if I can't prepare a meal. I just don't do it on a regular basis."

"When was the last time?" he asked.

She lifted her chin. "I prepared lunch for the twins just last week."

He laughed again, this time louder. "Bottles and jars of fruits and vegetables."

"They seemed to like it," she said. "Okay, what would you like for breakfast?"

"I'm guessing eggs Benedict would be too much to ask," he said.

She glowered at him.

"Okay. I'll go easy. Scrambled eggs, toast and coffee."

"I'll be right back with it," she said, muttering to herself as she continued down the rest of the stairs. This was ridiculous. Why should she care if Ryder considered her unskilled in the kitchen? He obviously respected her other talents such as organizing his childcare.

After a brief consultation with the sitter, however,

Bridget burned everything, even the coffee. She cleaned up her mess and started over, this time cooking everything on low. It seemed to take forever, but she finally got the job done and took the tray to Ryder's upstairs study.

He opened the door, wearing a distracted expression. "Thanks," he said, took the tray and closed the door.

She frowned, but took a breath. He was performing a difficult task. He needed understanding and patience.

Bridget went to his bedroom and arranged for a cleaning service. In her opinion, the house needed regular servicing. The sitters shouldn't be expected to clean in addition to keeping the twins. The twins were already a handful. An hour later, the cleaners arrived and she decided to take more coffee to Ryder.

She knocked on his door with the cup outstretched.

"Thanks," he said, still distracted as he accepted the cup. He closed the door again. She hesitated to interrupt, but thought it best to remove the dirty dishes, so she knocked again.

He opened the door, his eyebrows furrowed. "What?" he asked, almost in a curt voice.

"I thought I would take your dishes from breakfast," she said.

"Breakfast?" he said, his brow furrowing more.

"Yes, the eggs and toast you requested," she said.

"Oh," he said and went into his office. Seconds later, he returned with his uneaten eggs and toast.

"You didn't touch them," she said.

"Yeah, sorry. I'm really hung up over this eulogy."

Her frustration spiked. "I fixed these eggs and you didn't take a bite."

"I apologize. Really," he said, his face grief-stricken. In another instance, she would have screamed. But she knew Ryder was suffering.

"Fine," she managed in a tight voice. "What would you like for lunch?"

"Oh, anything. A ham sandwich. Thanks, *B*," he said and closed his door again. *B?* She'd never been called *B* in her life.

She helped the sitter with the boys, then took another trip to Ryder's study with a ham sandwich.

"Thanks," he said and accepted the sandwich.

"Are you okay?" she asked before he could close the door in her face.

He shook his head. "I'm not there yet." He leaned forward and pressed a quick kiss against her mouth.

After that brief meeting, Bridget left because she sensed Ryder needed his space and she was determined to respect it.

Ryder finally finished writing the eulogy. He had no idea what time it was until he glanced at the clock. 4:30 p.m. Whoa. Later than he intended. Good thing he'd cancelled all his appointments and that this wasn't a surgery day. Stretching his neck, he glanced around the room and noticed the sad-looking ham sandwich on the table on the other side of the room.

His heart swelled at the thought of Bridget bringing him food, reaching out to him. Taking the plate, he walked downstairs expecting to see the fresh, sexy face of Bridget Devereaux.

Instead he was greeted by Marshall.

"Hey, dude," he said. "How's it going?"

"Okay," he said. "The twins?"

"Down for a nap," Marshall said.

"Bridget?"

Marshall lifted a brow and smoothed back his hair with his hand. "She was here?"

"Yeah. She fixed me breakfast and a sandwich for lunch," Ryder said, frowning.

"Breakfast," Marshall repeated.

Reluctant to reveal details about his relationship with Bridget, he shrugged. "She showed up early. You should know. You told her about Dr. Walters. I was working on his eulogy."

Marshall winced. "Sorry, bro. I'm guessing she left a while ago. The sitter didn't say anything about her."

Ryder's gut tightened. "Okay, I guess she had other things to do."

"Well, she *is* a princess," Marshall said.

"Yeah," Ryder said.

"You're starting to fall for her, aren't you?" Marshall asked.

"Hell no."

Chapter Seven

"Dr. Walters was more than a brilliant doctor. He was a father figure to many of us who'd never known a father. He was an advocate at the same time that he demanded the best of every resident who crossed his path. He was the best man I've ever known," Ryder said and glanced at the large group who had gathered to remember Dr. Walters.

His gaze skimmed the crowd and stumbled over a classy young woman wearing a black hat and black dress. *Bridget.* Her presence gave him a potent shot of strength.

He continued with the rest of his eulogy, then made his way toward Bridget. The seat beside her was empty. Her eyes widened as he stepped in from the aisle.

"Thanks," he whispered, sitting down and clasping her hand between them.

"There was no other choice than to be here for you," she whispered.

His heart swelled at her words and he squeezed her hand, trying to remember the last time someone had been there for him like this. No expectation, just support and some kind of emotion close to love. Yet it couldn't be love, he told himself.

Her hand, however, sure felt great inside his.

A couple hours later, Ryder and Bridget joined Mrs. Walters for an afternoon meal. Dr. Walters's widow seemed to have aged a decade within the last year.

"You were his favorite," she said to Ryder, her eyes full of pain as she smiled. "He wasn't supposed to have a favorite, but he did."

Ryder's heart squeezed tight. "He was the father I never had. He challenged me and empathized with me. He made me want to be my best."

Mrs. Walters nodded. "He was an inspiring man."

"I'm lucky that he was my mentor," Ryder said.

Mrs. Walters nodded and frowned. "He was a wonderful, wonderful man. But we never had children. Our family life was always dependent on his schedule." She paused. "If there was one thing he might have changed before he…went away…" She swallowed over her grief. "I think he may have spent more time with his family. Me. His brothers and sister. Until he began to fade, he didn't realize how important relationships were." She closed her eyes for a moment, then shrugged. "I'm rambling." She patted Ryder's hand. "Never forget that you are more than that hospital. Never," she said.

Shaken by her fervent expression, he took a quick breath. "I won't," he said.

Within a half hour, he escorted Bridget to his car. "Come back to my house," he said.

She paused a half beat, then nodded. "Yes."

Moments later, they walked into his house. The sitter sat on the couch reading a book. "Hi," she said. "Everything go okay? The twins are sleeping and they've been no trouble."

"Good to hear it," he said. "I'm gonna change my clothes. Will you be here for a while?"

The sitter nodded. "I'm scheduled to be here till six. Then I have a class."

"Thanks," he said and turned to Bridget. "There's a place I want to take you."

"If it involves hiking or swimming, I'll need to change clothes," she warned him.

"You'll be okay."

Seven minutes later, he pulled in front of a waterfall fountain. Man-made but spectacular.

"It's beautiful," she said as they walked close to the fall and lifted her face to the spray. "Have you been here often?"

"Yes," he said, squeezing her hand.

"I can see why," she concluded and closed her eyes. "Whenever I have a few minutes near water, it reminds me of Chantaine. For all my complaining about being chained there the last year, I can't deny the effect water has on me. Makes me wonder if I have a gill somewhere. What about you?" she asked. "You've been landlocked most of your life, haven't you?"

"Yes, but I find that spending some time near water,

and I mean more than a shower or swimming pool, balances me out. Especially if something is bothering me."

"It's natural that Dr. Walters's passing would upset you," she said.

"It's more than that," he said. "Now that he is really gone, his position with the residents will need to be filled."

"You want it very much, don't you?" she asked.

Ryder felt torn in two completely opposing directions. "I feel a huge responsibility. The other doctor who would want the job comes off as callous. He doesn't care about helping residents with problems. His first instinct would be to cut them from the program. Dr. Walters probed deeper before making that kind of decision and he made himself available to residents for conference. The goal at our hospital is to approach the physician as a complete person so that he or she, in turn, treats the patient as a complete person."

"The doctors in your program are very fortunate to receive that kind of benefit, but based on what Dr. Walters's wife said, it must be difficult for the adviser to strike the balance as a complete person." She sighed. "In a different way, serving our country as royals can be an all-consuming proposition. Makes you wonder if there's such a thing as balance outside of a yoga class."

Her yoga reference made him smile. "How is it you can make me feel better on such a dark day?"

"One of my many delightful skills." She glanced again at the fountain. "Have you ever wanted to jump in one of these and get completely wet?"

"Yes," he said. "Where I was raised we had a small

fountain in the town in front of a bank. When I was a little boy, I jumped in it and stomped around. Got a paddling that kept me from sitting down for a week."

"Was it worth it?" she asked.

"Before and during, yes. Afterward no."

"I almost took the plunge once in Italy, but I knew I would be arrested and there would be a big fuss."

"So you restrained yourself," he said.

She frowned. "Yes, but one day. Maybe soon after I'm able to bring back some doctors to Chantaine and I take my long vacation in Italy..."

"Is that why you're in such a rush to import doctors?"

"Trust me, I've earned this break. Even Stefan agrees, but he and I both know Chantaine needs doctors. After my sister-in-law was injured so horribly while saving my life, it became even more clear. I still—"

The darkness in his eyes surprised him. "You don't still hold yourself responsible, do you?"

She paused a half beat too long. "Of course not. The gang stampeded her. Even security was taken by surprise," she said as if by rote.

"But you still feel responsible," he said.

"She wouldn't have been there if I hadn't begged her to join me," she said. "For someone to put her life on the line for me, and it wasn't as if she had taken an oath to protect me. She just did it because of who she is."

"And because of who you are," he said.

"Now that's a stretch," she said. "I spend a lot of time at charity events and school and business openings. It's not as if I'm in a research laboratory finding cures for dreadful diseases."

"No, but you're helping raise money for those

research scientists, and someone needs to do it. Don't underestimate your importance. You inspire people to give more than they usually would."

"Perhaps," she said, but clearly wasn't convinced. "Now I just need to find a way to inspire doctors to come to Chantaine. At least I've already got one specialist willing to hold seminars," she said, then shook her head. "But today isn't about me or Chantaine. It's about you, Ryder. How else can I help you with your grief?" she asked in a solemn tone.

His mind raced in a totally different direction down a path filled with hot kisses and hot bodies pressed against each other. He couldn't help but remember the sight of her naked body in his bed. He couldn't help but want her again.

Her eyes widened as if she could read his mind. "You're not serious," she said. "Men. Sex is the solution for everything."

"There are worse ways to deal with grief," he said.

"True, but with the sitter at your house, it would be difficult to indulge that particular solution," she said.

"You're right," he said. "I should get back to the hospital. I canceled my schedule for the rest of the day, but making up for a lost day is hell."

"Absolutely not," she said, then bit her lip. "I suppose we could go to my suite."

His gut twisted at the prospect of holding her again. He didn't understand his draw to Bridget. All he knew was that his life had seemed full of darkness and when he was with her, he felt lighter. With his demanding schedule, he felt as if he needed to snatch whatever stolen moments he could with her. "That's an invitation I can't imagine turning down," he said, sliding his fingers over a silky strand of her hair.

Her breath hitched and he found the response gratifying and reassuring. He was damn glad to know he wasn't the only one feeling this crazy attraction.

After an afternoon spent drowning his devils in Bridget's bed, a cell-phone alarm sounded.

"Time to go," Bridget said, then rubbed her mouth against his cheek and pulled away.

He caught her just before she rose from the bed. "What's the rush?"

"It's five-thirty. The sitter will be leaving at six," she said with a soft smile and pulled on a robe.

"Damn, it's that late?" He glanced at the alarm clock beside the bed to confirm her announcement and shook his head. He raked his hand through his hair. "Hey, come back to the house with me. We can get something delivered."

"I'm sorry, I can't. I have a previous commitment this evening. I'm attending a forum to promote the prevention of gang violence. As I'm sure you can imagine, this is a cause near and dear to my heart. The Dallas district attorney will escort me," she said.

Ryder's gut gave a vicious twist. He'd heard the current D.A. was quite the lady's man. "I'm guessing Corbin made those arrangements," he said, unable to keep his disapproval from his tone.

"I believe he did. I'm only using a part-time assistant while I'm in Texas, but the arrangements went through her. She left me a dossier on him, but I've been too busy to scan it."

"I can tell you what you need to know," he said rising from the bed. "Aiden Corbin was elected two years ago and is a hound dog when it comes to women."

"What exactly is a hound dog?" she asked.

Ryder scowled. "It's a man who will do just about anything to get women into his bed."

"Is that so?" she said and shot a sideways glance at him. "It seems to me I've met several *hound dogs* here in Dallas."

"Hey, I'm no hound dog. I'm a hardworking doctor trying to take care of my brother's twin babies."

"It's really hard for me to buy your defense with you standing naked in front of me," she said, her glance falling over him in a hot wave that made it hard for him to resist pulling her right back into bed.

"I'm not used to being with a woman who has to fight off my competitors with a stick," he said.

She blinked. "Competitors," she echoed. "That would suggest I view these men on the same level as you, which I don't."

"What level is that?"

She paused then frowned. "Different. Besides, I don't have to beat the men off with a stick. And you must remember their primary attraction to me is due to my title and perhaps the erroneous view that I'm loaded."

"You underestimate your appeal."

"Hmm," she said. "Minus my title, I'm extremely average."

"You're wrong," he retorted. "You're beautiful and talented. You're...magic," he said, surprising himself with his words. Even though they were all true, they weren't the kinds of things he would usually say.

Bridget paused. Her eyes shimmering with emotion, she threw herself against him and wrapped her arms around him. “That’s the nicest thing anyone has ever said to me. I’m not sure I agree, but it’s quite wonderful that you would actually think those things about me. Thank you, Ryder. I will cherish your words forever,” she said, then pulled away.

Something about her thank-you reminded him that his relationship with Bridget was temporary. That was fine with him. Lord knew, with everything on his plate, he didn’t have time for a real relationship with a woman. For that matter, he’d never taken time to have a *real* relationship with a woman. He’d always been too busy with his career. So this relationship was no different, he told himself, but something about that didn’t settle right with him.

That night, after he’d tucked the twins into their cribs and watched the rest of the ball game, he half glanced at the local news. Just as he was about to switch the channel, a video of Bridget and the D.A. appeared.

“Her Royal Highness, Bridget Devereaux of Chantaine, accompanied Dallas’s district attorney, Aiden Corbin, to a special discussion at the Dallas Forum tonight. Reporter Charles Pine reports.”

“Your Highness, welcome to Dallas. I’m curious, how can a small, idyllic island like Chantaine have a gang problem?”

“My country is quite idyllic, and we’re quite fortunate that we have only occasionally had problems with gangs. Still, there have been incidents, and we are always exploring ways to prevent such problems in the future. Mr. Corbin has generously offered to present his experiences and knowledge by visiting our country in the future."

"Sounds like a rough gig, Mr. Corbin," the reporter joked.

Corbin gave a wide smile that looked lecherous to Ryder. "The princess is being very generous with her public and charitable appearances while she visits our city. The least I can do is to share my expertise in return."

Ryder bet the D.A. wanted to share more than his expertise. His stomach burned from the pizza he'd eaten earlier. His cell phone rang and he saw the caller ID belonged to Marshall.

Ryder answered the call, but Marshall started talking before he could open his mouth.

"Hey, what's your babe doing with our slimeball D.A.?"

"It's just business," he said, grinding his teeth at the same time.

"Business with the horn dog of the century?" Marshall asked. "If she was my woman, I wouldn't let her anywhere near Corbin."

Ryder bit his tongue. He'd had the same strange primitive reaction, but he had to contain himself.

"Whoa," Marshall said after the short silence. "You didn't say anything. Does that mean she's fair game? Because I gotta tell you that's one sweet piece of—"

"Don't even think about it," Ryder said. "With a sharp knife, I could disembowel you in less than sixty seconds."

Marshall gave a dirty chuckle. "Gotcha. I was just

kidding. I'm focused on someone else. I could tell something was cooking between the two of you. The way you act about her. The way she acts about you."

"What do you mean the way she acts about me?"

"Well, she's busted her royal ass trying to make sure your boys have got good care," Marshall said. "Speaking of good care, I took a bucket of chicken to your nanny the other day. Seemed the charitable thing to do."

"You took food to Suzanne?" Ryder said. "I told you to leave her alone."

"It was just chicken. She's been recovering, for God's sake. Give the poor girl a break," Marshall said.

Ryder narrowed his eyes. "You don't deliver chicken unless you're hoping for something for yourself."

"I'm insulted," Marshall said. "I can be a nice guy. Listen, I don't have time for this. I'll just tell you that you might want to keep an eye on your little princess because Aiden Corbin is known for poaching. G'night, Mr. M.D."

Ryder opened his mouth to reply, but he knew Marshall had clicked off the call. Marshall had always called him Mr. M.D. when he thought Ryder was getting too big for his britches. Trouble was, what Marshall had said about Corbin was right. The other trouble was Ryder had no real claim on Bridget, so the only thing left for him to do was stew. No way, he told himself. There was no good reason to stew over a temporary woman. He'd never done it before, and he wasn't going to start now.

Bridget left two messages on Ryder's cell during the next two days, but he hadn't answered. She worried that something may have happened. What if there'd been a problem with the nanny? Had his workload tripled as a result of Dr. Walters's death? She already knew he'd been reluctant to touch base with her when things weren't going well, so she decided to make a quick trip to his office at the hospital.

He was in a meeting with a resident, but just as she started to leave a message with his assistant, the resident exited his office.

"I'll let him know you're here," his assistant said.

Another moment later, Ryder opened his door. "Come in," he said.

Wondering at his abrupt tone, she entered his office and watched as he closed the door behind her. "I was concerned when I didn't hear back from you. Is everything okay with you and the twins?"

"No problem," he said. "Suzanne returned to work and the boys seem to be fine."

She frowned at how remote he seemed. "Are you sure you're okay? You seem—"

"Busy," he said in a firm voice.

"Well, I didn't mean to bother you," she said.

"I have another two or three minutes," he said.

Her jaw dropped of its own volition. "Excuse me?"

"I said I have another two or three minutes. Then I need to go to a meeting."

"Why are you acting this way?" she demanded.

"What way?"

"As if we're strangers," she said. "As if we've never shared a bed."

His eyes suddenly darkened with turmoil. "We don't have a committed relationship."

Bridget's heart twisted. She felt as if he'd slapped her. "Does that mean you have to act rude and uncaring?"

He paused. "No, but we both know this isn't a long-term relationship. You have your reasons. I have mine. There's no need to pretend anything different."

If she felt he'd slapped her before, she now felt he'd stabbed her. "I wasn't pretending. I was just caring," she said. "Clearly a mistake," she said and turned toward the door.

He grabbed her arm just before she reached the doorknob.

She turned, feeling more confused than she could remember in her life. "Why are you acting this way?"

"Our relationship isn't normal," he said.

"Well, you're not normal and neither am I, so why should it be?"

"I have no right to comment on what men you spend time with," he said

Realization swept over her. "Oh, for bloody sakes, is this about the D.A.?"

"Saw you on the news," he said. "He was trying hard."

"And got nowhere," she said. "Do you really think I would hop into bed with him after I'd just been with you? Do you really think I would hop into bed with anyone? You must think I'm the most promiscuous woman ever born."

"You get a lot of offers," he said and she could see he was torn. He was accustomed to being in control and now he wasn't.

"I get offers because I'm a princess, not because I'm me," she said.

"Not—"

She shook her head. "Okay, we'll have to agree to disagree. Again. The point is I haven't engaged in a meaningless affair, well, ever," she said. "It's just not my nature. And my affair, I'm not sure I like that word. My relationship with you isn't meaningless. I don't exactly know what it means because you and I seem to be headed in different directions. But I'm incredibly drawn to you. I can't explain it and I don't particularly like it. It's bloody well inconvenient, but damn it, you're important to me."

He stared at her for a long moment, then gave a short, humorless laugh. "Ditto."

"What does that mean?"

"Exactly what you said. I'm willing to ride this horse to the end of this race if you are."

Bridget had to digest his words. She wasn't accustomed to such references.

"I mean we'll take it till the end and then kiss each other good-bye," he said.

The word good-bye bothered her, but she didn't feel as if she had any other choice.

"Deal?" he asked, extending his hand.

She slowly placed her hand in his. "Deal."

He pulled her against him. "Come over tonight," he said.

Her heart slammed against her rib cage. "I'd like to, but I have a previous engagement."

"Damn," he said. "Just tell me it's not with Aiden Corbin."

She shook her head. "It's with the head of Pediatrics."

Ryder swore. "That's better?"

"You told me if I bring medical experts to Chantaine to do temporary training, then I'll have a better chance of attracting doctors."

"Why can't you choose old, married experts?" he grumbled.

She smiled. "Introduce me."

He lowered his head and gave her a long kiss that made her head spin.

When he pulled back, they were both breathing hard. "What about tomorrow night?"

"I have an engagement," she said. "But I'll rearrange it."

"Okay. Tomorrow night is another water class for the twins. I'll order takeout for us." He gave her a quick firm kiss. "You'd have more fun with me than the Pediatrics department head tonight."

Ryder arrived home a few minutes late that night to find Marshall's truck parked in front of his house. He opened his front door to find Marshall bouncing Tyler on his knee while Suzanne was changing Travis's diaper.

Tyler squealed. Marshall grinned. "Looks like somebody's glad to see you," he said and immediately handed the baby to Ryder.

Ryder's heart lifted at the baby's obvious joy and he kissed him on his soft cheek. Travis also gave an earsplitting shriek.

Suzanne glanced up at him. "I've already fed them, but they're a little worked up. That may be due to Marshall," she said with a faintly accusing expression.

"Hey, I was just entertaining them until you got

home," Marshall said and picked up Travis. "I thought I'd try to give Suzanne a break from the heavy lifting."

Uh-huh, Ryder thought. "It's okay. I'm glad they're in a good mood. Can you give me a quick minute to talk to Marshall?"

"Of course," Suzanne said. "There's no rush. And if you want to change clothes, I can wait for that, too."

"Thanks," he said and gave a sharp jerk of his head to go outside to Marshall.

Ryder carried Tyler in his arms and Marshall carried Travis. "What the hell do you think you're doing?" Ryder demanded.

"Hey, I'm just helping out your nanny. You don't want another one to quit because of these wild boys, do you?"

"Suzanne had no intention of quitting. She's just recovering from her appendectomy," Ryder said.

"All the more reason for me to stop by and help her. These boys are getting bigger every day."

"She doesn't need your help."

"Says who?" Marshall challenged.

"Says me," Ryder retorted. "You just want to get into her pants."

Marshall shot him a quelling glare that would have worked with any other man.

Not Ryder. "Stay away from my nanny."

"You're just edgy because you're not getting any," Marshall said.

"That's none of your damn business," Ryder said.

"It is if it makes you act like a jerk," Marshall said, then sucked in a quick breath. "Listen, I like Suzanne. I think she likes me. I wanna give this a try."

"She's not your kind of woman," Ryder said.

"Well, maybe I've been going after the wrong kind of woman."

Ryder groaned. "If you wreck my nanny, I'll kill you."

"Give me a chance," Marshall said. "She is."

Ryder swore under his breath. "Okay, but if you mess up her mind..."

"Yeah, yeah, yeah," Marshall said. "When are you supposed to see your princess again? For the sake of all of us, I hope it's soon."

Filled with misgivings, Ryder watched his nanny drive off in Marshall's wake to a restaurant. Maybe he was just jealous, a voice inside him said, and he brushed it aside. The boys were rowdy and demanding and absorbed every ounce of his energy by the time they fell asleep.

When he awakened the following morning to the sound of Travis screaming at the top of his lungs, he could have sworn it was the middle of the night. Instead, it was 6:30 a.m.

Stumbling into the twins' bedroom, he picked up the baby and held him against him. "Hey, bud, what's up? You're okay."

Travis's cry melted to a whimper, and Ryder sensed the baby was missing his real father and mother. The thought twisted his gut. Poor kid would never know his real dad and mom. He was stuck with Ryder, and Ryder knew he would never be the father his brother would have been.

Chapter Eight

Later that morning, Ryder joined the chief of staff with Dr. Hutt in a meeting to discuss the future of the adviser program.

"There's been some debate over how we should continue this program in the future now that Dr. Walters is no longer with us," the chief of staff said.

"It's one of the things about our program that makes it distinctive and appealing to residents," Ryder said. "I can't imagine changing it."

"I agree that the program should continue," the chief said. "But Dr. Walters was one of a kind and we may need to make changes."

"Not if those changes will negatively impact the residents," Ryder countered.

"The residents needed to be toughened," Hutt said. "They've chosen the medical profession. It's a demanding field, so they need to be ready to take on their jobs.

Long hours and dedication to excelling in their fields are critical."

"They also need to deal with their patients as individuals. We enforce that teaching by treating them as individuals," Ryder said, feeling his back get up, ready for a fight.

"You're too soft on them," Hutt said.

"You treat them like a machine because that's how you treat your patients," Ryder said.

"Gentlemen," the chief of staff intervened. "There's no need for insults."

Ryder resisted the urge to glare at him and took a quick breath. "Forgive me," he said. "But Dr. Walters was very important to me. It would be an insult to him if I didn't present his point of view in this discussion."

"And you think I'm not," Hutt said. "Dr. Walters was my adviser, too. I worshipped the ground he walked on. What he taught me was the importance of discipline."

Ryder couldn't disagree. Discipline was critical to a doctor's success. "I've never disagreed with the importance of discipline, but Dr. Walters also emphasized to me to remember the human element."

"You're both right," the chief said. "And you've both clearly demonstrated your superior ability as medical doctors. The difficulty is that Dr. Walters spent an unbelievable amount of time counseling residents at the same time he managed his patient load. There was rarely a time he wasn't here at the hospital. Neither of you can make that kind of time commitment."

"I have a very understanding wife."

"I have a perfect nanny."

"Therefore," the chief of staff said. "I am going to assign both of you as intern advisers."

That sounded like a horrible idea to Ryder. "I can't imagine that Dr. Walters would approve."

"Unfortunately, Dr. Walters isn't here to give his advice. I agree that the advisership is one of the unique features of our program, but I can't in good conscience assign the total advisership to you, Dr. McCall, given your new family obligations."

"The two of you will have to work together or I will find new advisers," the chief continued. "The three of us will meet in two weeks."

Ryder led the way out the door, barely resisting the urge to slam it shut behind him. "This is a joke," he muttered.

"Hey, I don't want to work with you either. Just because you were Gordon's favorite doesn't mean the rest of us didn't see how great he was. And don't try to deny it. How did you get the financial relief you needed when your mother was dying?" he challenged.

Ryder's fingers itched to punch Hutt in his face. "He pointed me in the direction of several teaching opportunities. One of them worked out. It was that or wait tables. How did *you* get through med school?"

"You know how I got through. My parents paid for me. I started partying a little too much once I graduated and he told me I had to toe the line or go somewhere else. Rode my butt every time I walked into the hospital. I learned the hard way the importance of discipline."

"I did, too. I just learned it about ten years earlier than you did because I had to," he said and turned away.

Hutt caught his arm. "Just curious, what would it

take for you to give up the advisership and let me take it over?"

"A miracle," Ryder said.

"Too vague. I can't shoot for that," he said.

His colleague's response took him by surprise. "You gotta understand the guys who don't have parents who can pay their way. You gotta understand the guys who don't get into school because their daddy knows somebody. I'm not sure you can get there. Ever."

"You're an ass," Hutt said.

"So are you," Ryder said.

"Maybe that's why the chief is making us work together."

"Unless he's hoping we'll kill each other," Ryder muttered and went to his office.

That night, although Ryder physically did everything the teachers instructed them to do with the babies, Bridget could tell his mind was somewhere else. She tried not to focus on it as she watched Tyler put his face in the water and blow bubbles.

"Good boy," she said, praising the baby. "Good for you. Such a brave, brilliant boy."

Travis must have taken a competitive cue because he plunged his face in the water and lifted it, choking. Frightened, he began to cry.

"Oh no, that water went down the wrong way," she said, passing Tyler to Ryder and holding out her hands for Travis. "Poor thing. No need to go diving," she gently chastised him. "Watch," she said and lowered her mouth to the water and blew bubbles.

Ryder followed her lead and blew bubbles, making a sound with his deeper voice.

Travis quickly dried up and stared.

"Do it again," she said.

Ryder repeated and Travis let out a belly laugh.

Bridget couldn't resist laughing, too. "What a brilliant sound," she said. "Do it again."

Ryder dipped his head and shot her a dark, mocking look. "Yes, Your Majesty." He blew bubbles and this time, both Travis and Tyler laughed.

"Well done," she said. "Just a couple more times."

"Want to give it another go?" she asked Travis. "We can do it together." She lowered her mouth to the water to blow bubbles. "Come on."

Holding him securely, she dipped his chin in the water. He made a motorboat sound with his lips. Slowly, she lowered his mouth and he made the same sound. Just before he breathed in water, she pulled up his chin, and again he let out a belly laugh.

"Good boy," she said. "Brilliant."

"You never say that to me," Ryder muttered.

"Perhaps you need to try harder," she retorted.

He groaned and she felt his gaze sweep over her body with a flash of instant need before he hid it. 'You could drive a man insane, Your Majesty," he said.

"Your Majesty is incorrect. If you're going to address me correctly, you should say Your Highness. Or if you want to irritate me, you could use the term my brother-in-law's housekeeper uses. Your Highliness."

"I like that," he said. "Has a nice ring to it. Your Highliness."

She scowled. "So what put you in a bad mood at

work? Did one of your patients develop a secondary infection?"

"Hell no," he said frowning. "How did you know something happened at work?"

She rolled her eyes. "Because you're here and not here at the same time. You do everything the teachers say, but you're not really here. Some women would be insulted."

"It's probably best if I'm not completely here because looking at you in that bathing suit could make things embarrassing for me when I step out of the pool. But because you asked, there are some complications with the resident advisory position. I have to deal with the equivalent of the M.D. devil."

She winced. "That can't be enjoyable. Then again, would he be easier to deal with than you?"

He shot her a deadly look. "If you don't mind dealing with someone who will lie to your face."

She frowned. "Bloody hell for both of us," she muttered under her breath.

The teacher ended the class and Bridget and Ryder climbed out of the pool with the boys. Bridget changed Travis's drenched diaper while Ryder changed Tyler's. "You and your brother are the most brilliant, fabulous boys in the world. Never doubt it," she said and rubbed her nose against Travis's.

The baby laughed and grabbed at her. Her heart twisted in her chest. "So sweet."

"You're good with them," Ryder said.

"Shocking, isn't it?" she said.

"I think both of them have a crush on you," he said, leaning toward her. "Or maybe all three of us."

She smiled, feeling a surprising flood of warmth flow inside her. "You think they really like me? I've never thought of myself as good with babies."

Travis pressed a wet, open-mouth kiss against her cheek.

"Yeah, they clearly hate you," Ryder said.

She sighed. "I never thought I could adore babies this much."

"Me either," he said, drawing Tyler against him. The baby snuggled against him. "Not sure about this fatherhood thing. I didn't have the best example."

"Neither did I," she said. "He couldn't ever remember my name."

"You're joking," he said, disturbed by the complacent expression on her face.

She shrugged. "My mother's job was to reproduce. There were a bonus of girls. She stopped after the second son which was after Phillipa and me."

"You weren't close to your mom either, were you?" he guessed.

"Hers wasn't a happy marriage. My mother had high hopes when she married my father, but she ended up terribly disappointed. So yes, I'm ill-prepared to be a loving mother. The only part of my background that gives me hope is my siblings. Stefan and Tina were more like parents to me."

"I guess that's another thing we have in common. We didn't have the best parents in the world. We were just on opposite ends of the spectrum. Yours were royal. Mine were dirt-poor," he said. "How did I get lucky enough to have a princess half-naked in a pool with me?"

"And your twin boys," she added, laughing. "I'm glad they like me. It's amazing how they get under your skin."

"Yeah," he said, looking down at Tyler. "I just hope I can figure out how to keep them safe, happy and feeling like they can conquer the world."

"I think you will," she said. "If anyone can, you can."

"The great thing about the swimming class is that it totally wears out the boys and they sleep like babies should," Ryder said, sitting on the couch beside Bridget with his hand wrapped around hers. "The bad thing is that it wears me out, too."

She gave a low, throaty chuckle that grabbed at his gut. "Times ten," she said.

"If you're as tired as I am, then you better stay the night," he said.

She slid him a sideways glance. "My driver could take me home. It would be no problem."

"Maybe not for him, but it would be for me," he said, drawing her head toward his and taking her mouth in a long kiss.

When he pulled away, Bridget sighed. The sound was magic to him. He couldn't get enough of her and he hated himself for it, yet he couldn't avoid it.

"Does that mean you'll stay the night?" he asked. "I can promise I'll wake you up in the middle of the night."

She lifted her hand to the back of his head and drew his lips to hers. "Just do your best," she said and he vowed he would.

The next morning, Bridget awakened to the sound of babies crying and the sight of an empty bed. She'd stayed the night with Ryder, and he had apparently left early this morning. Pulling one of his shirts around her and buttoning it, she walked toward the nursery.

Walking inside, she nearly bumped into Suzanne.

"Oh, please excuse me," Bridget said, covering a yawn.

Suzanne yawned in response. "No problem," she said. "I arrived a little late and Dr. McCall left right out the door."

"He has a lot on his mind," Bridget said.

Suzanne nodded. "I can tell. You can go back to bed. I can handle the boys."

"No, I'll carry him downstairs," Bridget said, changing Travis, then picking him up and holding him against her. "No need to cry. You're probably still tired from all that swimming."

"They can steal your heart pretty quickly, can't they?" Suzanne asked, smiling at Bridget as she cuddled the baby.

"Yes, I never dreamed I could feel this much affection for two little semi-humans who spit peas at you, scream bloody murder and can get downright stinky. Whenever anyone asked me how I felt about babies, I always thought they were fine if they belonged to someone else."

"I was just the opposite," Suzanne said. "I wanted to have children, but I couldn't. My husband felt the same way. That's a big part of the reason he left."

Saddened by Suzanne's confession, Bridget frowned as she followed the nanny downstairs. "But there are other ways, adoption, surrogacy…."

"He wanted children the natural way," Suzanne said.

"I'm sorry. It was clearly his loss. I have to believe there's a better man in your future," Bridget said.

Suzanne's cheeks turned pink. "Maybe, but I'll never marry again. The ending was just too painful. What about you? Is marriage in your future?" she asked as if she wanted the attention diverted away from her.

Bridget blinked, uncomfortable with the question, so she gave her automatic response as she put Travis into a high chair. "No time soon. Italy is calling me first, and then we'll see."

"What about Dr. McCall?"

"Oh, he's not interested in marriage. He has his hands full with the boys and his practice and the residents at the hospital. I'm certain it's not in his plans to marry anytime soon."

"Plans can change in an instant," Suzanne said. "I bet he didn't plan to be a daddy to twins either."

"So true," Bridget agreed, growing more uncomfortable with the conversation with each passing second. "It's definitely been a shock. That's enough of an adjustment without adding a wife into the mix."

"Hmm," Suzanne said as if she didn't quite agree but wouldn't say more.

Bridget felt a rush of relief. "Can you handle the feeding? I'd like to take a shower."

"No problem. Take your time," Suzanne said.

As Bridget stepped under the warm spray of water in Ryder's shower, she smelled the scent of his soap and felt surrounded by him again. She wondered if she and Ryder were making a mistake by becoming involved. She preferred the notion that her attraction to him was strong but temporary; however, between her surprising, growing feelings for the babies and her assignment to set up a program for doctors to Chantaine, their relationship was complicated at best.

Bridget dressed and allowed her hair to air-dry with the plan to perform her daily makeover at her hotel suite. She lingered at Ryder's house, playing with the twins until her phone rang and it was Stefan.

Her stomach sank with dread at the prospect of talking to her brother. So far, she'd successfully avoided speaking to him directly by keeping him apprised via email. Stefan was a wonderful, good-intentioned but interfering brother, and because he was crown prince, he could get more than a bit bossy. His new wife, Eve, had helped to rein him in, but the man had been born to rule. Some traits could never be eradicated.

"Hello, Stefan. My, you're up late. How are you?" she asked, moving away from the twins so he wouldn't hear them in the background.

"I'm fine. I need to discuss the progress with the doctor program—"

Tyler let out a loud scream as Bridget left his sight. Bridget winced, walking quickly toward one of the downstairs bathrooms and closing the door.

"What was that? It sounded like a wild animal," he said.

Close enough, she thought ruefully. "It was a baby. I guess it's naptime. Now, regarding the doctor program, I've hit a snag with—"

"Baby," he echoed. "What are you doing with a baby? You don't like children."

"I don't dislike children," she said. "I've just never spent much time with them. That was a twin infant I met by chance. I've gotten to know the family because they've had a bit of a crisis. Everything is headed in the right direction now, though. About the doctors for Chantaine—"

"This wouldn't be one of Dr. Ryder McCall's twin nephews, would it? Valentina told me you've been spending quite a bit of time with Dr. McCall and his children."

Valentina had snitched on her. She would have to be more careful what she said to her sister. "It turns out Dr. McCall is the resident adviser for the Texas Medical Center. I've been trying to persuade him to participate in our program, but he says that working on Chantaine isn't prestigious enough because we don't already have any specialized programs or research in place."

"Chantaine, not prestigious enough," he said, his tone dripping with fury.

Bridget had indicated that she'd not made as much progress as she wanted because the head adviser was ill and the hospital was undergoing transition, which was partly true. She'd hoped she wouldn't have to tell Stefan the full truth because she'd known he would be offended. "I reacted the same way. Told him he was the most insulting man I'd ever met. Now to accomplish my task, I'm stuck trying to get him to compromise," she said with sigh.

Silence followed. "Bridget, you're not trying to use seduction as a way of convincing the man, are you?"

Bridget laughed, partly from hilarity, partly from hysteria. If Stefan only knew. Heaven help her if he did. Then again, Raoul would talk if pressed. "If only it were that easy," she said. "The man is almost as stubborn as you are," she said.

Another silence passed, and Bridget could feel her brother's tension through the phone line. "That doesn't bode well for our plan. You've begun to approach other hospitals."

"Yes, I have, but I'm getting similar, though more politely worded, responses. Because of that, I've begun to invite various high-level doctors to Chantaine to conduct training and seminars. So far, three doctors have committed."

"Excellent," he said. "We may need to expand our search."

"I know. I'm hopeful that if I can recruit some additional specialists that we'll be able to overcome the objections of our top choices for hospitals," she said.

"Bridget," he said. "I know that part of the reason you feel strongly about this is because of what happened to Eve," he said.

"Of course I do. Thank goodness she received the care she needed in time."

"I feel the same way. Just keep your meetings businesslike," he said.

Bridget frowned. "What do you mean?"

"I mean, you can be charming and you're young and attractive. These men could become enamored with the idea of seducing a princess. I wouldn't want your reputation to suffer as a result of any misplaced determination."

"Now, I believe I'm insulted. Do you really believe I'm so easily swayed? And do you think this is the first time I haven't had to put up with unwanted advances?"

"There's no reason for you to be insulted. I'm just looking out for you. What do you mean, unwanted advances?" he demanded. "Raoul is supposed to stay on top of that."

"Unless you have something further to say that could be construed as helpful, I believe we've spoken long enough. I have things to do as I'm sure you do, too."

"Bridget, do not hang up on me. I'm not finished," her brother commanded.

She was tempted to push the button to disconnect. So tempted that her finger itched. "I'm waiting," she finally said.

"Phillipa is coming to Texas for a visit," he announced. "She's been acting depressed for the last few weeks and she's had a terrible time working on her dissertation. Eve thinks getting away from Chantaine and taking a break from her studies will help her."

Her stomach twisted in concern. "You don't think she's ill, do you?"

"No, she's been checked out by the royal doctors, but after Ericka's drug problems, I can't take any chances."

Alarm shot through Bridget. Her sister Ericka had become dependent on drugs and spent more than one stint in rehab. Thank goodness, she'd left her problems behind and she was now happily married to her French film-director husband. "I can't believe our Pippa would get involved with drugs. Not after how much all of us suffered when Ericka was having her problems."

"I don't think she is, but she's lost weight and seems miserable and distracted. A change of pace will refresh her."

"Between Valentina and me, we'll do our best," she promised.

"The initial plan is for her to spend most of her time at the ranch, but I'm sure she'll come into Dallas for a visit," he said.

"Yes," she said. "Thank you for letting me know. And how are Eve and Stephenia?"

"Eve is wonderful. Stephenia is a terror, but I swear I think she's already learning to read. Still quite demanding that I read to her every night if at all possible," he said, his tone a mixture of exasperation and tenderness.

"You're a lucky man, Stefan, to have a wife and daughter who love you," she said, then couldn't resist adding, "along with your loyal, subservient siblings."

He gave a short laugh. "Yes to both, although my siblings will never be subservient."

"It's not in our genes," she said. "Give my love to Eve and Stephenia."

"I will. And Bridget," he said, "if you can't work things out with this Dr. McCall soon, we'll move past him and onto someone more cooperative."

Bridget's stomach twisted at the thought. "I hear what you're saying."

"Good," he said. "All for now. We'll talk soon."

Bridget took a deep breath as the call was disconnected. Her mind raced with thoughts about Phillipa, Ryder and the twins, and her assignment to recruit new doctors to Chantaine. She grew dizzy under the opposing priorities and returned to the den with the idea of heading outside to clear her head.

On her way, however, Travis screeched at her.

"His version of hello?" she said to Suzanne.

"I think so," Suzanne said. "It's time for their morning nap and Tyler is almost there. Travis is next."

"I'll take him," Bridget said and went to the blanket on the floor to pick up the baby. "How are you doing, mister?"

He made an unintelligible sound and plastered his open mouth against her in a wet baby kiss.

Her heart turned over. "You're such a flirt," she accused in a voice she knew was far too affectionate.

He put an open-mouth kiss against her cheek again.

"Too much," she said and cuddled him.

Travis snuggled against her and sank his head against her throat. He sighed and seconds later, his breathing became more regular. Another half minute and she felt drool sliding down her neck.

It was the sweetest moment of her week. Or month. Or longer.

"You have a calming effect on him," Suzanne whispered. "He looks like he could sleep right there against you forever."

Travis sighed against her skin and she felt the terrible urge to tear up. Heaven help her, she needed to get her emotions under control.

Travis wiggled again and clung to her as if she were the most important person in the world. Her heart dipped at the way the baby made her feel. He was so vulnerable. She wanted to take care of him, make him feel safe…. Yet, he wasn't her baby.

Bridget savored his baby scent and the sensation of his healthy, chubby baby body in her arms. What an addictive combination. She wanted to hold him until nighttime…or later… Is this what happened to parents?

Perhaps this is why babies survived. They made you want to take care of them. Forever.

It took another few moments in the rocking chair, but Bridget finally decided Travis could hit the sack. She carried him upstairs to the nursery and gently placed him in his crib. Tyler was already asleep. Travis was the fussier baby. That should have made him less desirable, but Bridget considered it a challenge to comfort him and help him fall asleep.

"Very good for a princess," Suzanne said from the doorway. "Are you sure you don't have some magic you're hiding in your back pocket?"

Flattered, Bridget quietly stepped from the room and pulled the door shut behind her. "You should know better. The only magic with babies is if they feel safe."

"They both feel safe with you," Suzanne said.

Bridget's heart twisted. What did all of this mean? "I should go. I have appointments and phone conferences."

"Princess things to do," Suzanne said with a gentle smile.

Bridget nodded. "But if you have a problem with the twins, call me."

Suzanne sighed. "You hired me to take care of the twins. Yet you feel you need to help. Why is that?"

Bridget's stomach clenched again. "I'm not any kind of expert. It's like you said earlier. They sneak up on you and grab your heart."

Chapter Nine

After Bridget finally tore herself away from the babies, she threw herself into her task of soliciting visiting medical experts for Chantaine. It irritated her when the experts laughed off her proposal, but she persevered and won two maybes and one new definite yes for her efforts.

Between her schedule and Ryder's, they only managed text messages and a few phone calls. Although she was tired by bedtime, she was surprised at how much she missed Ryder and the boys. Just as she fell asleep, her cell phone rang. Her heart skipped at the caller ID.

"Hello," she said.

Before she could say another word, he said. "Dinner. Tomorrow night. 7:00 p.m. No excuses. It's been too long."

She laughed, crazy thrilled to hear his voice. "Oh my. Is it a doctor thing that you give orders like a royal?"

"Maybe," he said. "I can't talk. I've got to check on a patient," he said.

"This late?" she asked and heard the sound of voices in the background.

"He's diabetic and he's experiencing some complications from surgery. I'll stay another hour to make sure he's stable. Tomorrow night, I'm taking you out."

The next morning, soon after Bridget awakened, she received a call from her sister Tina. "We're coming to town for dinner tonight. You must join us."

"Oh no. I'm sorry, but I already have a commitment," Bridget said, immediately feeling edgy because she knew Tina had talked to Stefan.

"Is it business or pleasure? Because if it's pleasure, we can all go out together," Tina offered.

Bridget paused. Her dinner with Ryder promised pure pleasure, but if she discussed Chantaine's medical program, it could be construed as business.

"I can tell by your hesitation that it's pleasure," Tina said before Bridget could pull an excuse together. "We'll pick you up for a six-thirty dinner at the Longhorn Club."

"It'll have to be a 7:00 p.m. dinner," she automatically corrected. "Ryder has already set the time and I'm sure he'll be busy going from the hospital, home and back out again. In fact, this may not be such a good idea after all. He's extremely busy lately. I haven't seen him myself in three days."

"Three days," Tina repeated. "If that's such a long gap of time between your dates, then I would say the two of you are getting quite cozy. All the more reason for me to meet him."

Resenting her sister's interference, Bridget frowned. "And which member of the royal family gave your husband Zachary the stamp of approval while the two of you were seeing each other?"

"None, but my pregnancy put a different spin on the situation—" Tina gasped. "You're not pregnant, are you?"

"Of course not," Bridget said.

"But the two of you must be serious for you to get all snippy with me," Tina continued. "The only way you can disprove it is if you and your doctor meet Zach and me for dinner tonight. Ciao, darling," she said and hung up.

Bridget swore at the phone and tossed it on her bed. She didn't want to share Ryder with her sister or anyone else at the moment. She was appalled to admit, only to herself, that she'd missed Ryder and the twins terribly during the last few days. It had taken every bit of her self-control not to dash over to his house to hold the babies or to visit Ryder at the hospital. She knew, however, that she was growing entirely too attached to all three males. And now Ryder would have to face an inquisition from both her sister and her brother-in-law. She wouldn't blame Ryder if he ran screaming.

Deciding to give him the easy way out, she sent him a text message. *Change of plans. My sister and her husband insist we join them for dinner. I'll understand if you can't join us.*

When he didn't immediately answer, she suspected he was trying to word his response and took a shower, feeling glum, bordering pouty. Amazing how one phone call from her nosy sister could send her mood into the pits. When she got out of the shower, her cell phone dinged to indicate a message.

I'm in. Where?

Her heart turned cartwheels and she gave him the name of the restaurant along with a warning that her sister's interrogation could rival the American's CIA. Although she much preferred sharing an evening with Ryder without the company of her sister, she couldn't deny she was excited to get to see him, period.

That night, Bridget fought a surprising spate of nerves on the way to the restaurant. "Tell us more about your doctor," Tina said.

"You'll meet him soon enough," she said. "He's very work-oriented, but he's making adjustments now that he's the guardian for his twin infant nephews." She deliberately changed the subject. "Stefan told me Phillipa will be coming for a visit soon. He sounded worried. Have you had a chance to talk with her?"

"I've called, but she hasn't returned my call, which has me concerned. What about you?"

"I just left a message telling her I was looking forward to seeing her. She may need to relax a little before she's ready to talk. I didn't want to put any more pressure on her. I wondered if it was related to her studies, but Phillipa has always thrived under academic pressure."

"I think a little quiet time at our ranch will help her and we can come into town for a little fun. Of course, you could spend more time at the ranch, too," Tina said in a pointed voice.

"I have a task to complete and I can't do it from the

ranch," Bridget said, refusing to give in to her sister's dig. "Now I'm in the process of trying to lure medical specialists to come to Chantaine so we can attract more medical doctors to our program."

"And what about your Dr. McCall? How would he feel about visiting Chantaine?"

Bridget laughed at the thought, yet felt a twinge of sadness at the same time. "He's far too busy with his work at the hospital and with the twins. I can't imagine his even considering it."

"Oh, I don't know," Tina said. "Maybe because the two of you are so close—"

"Not that close," Bridget said flatly.

"If you're looking for doctors who would like to combine a vacation with teaching in Chantaine, I might know a few," Zachary offered.

"Oh, that would be fabulous. Please do let me know of any of your connections," Bridget said.

"Zachary recruited an obstetrician to the small town close to the ranch, so he might be able to give you some tips," Tina said.

"Part of it is finding the right person. Not every doctor wants to practice in a big city hospital. You may have your heart set on Texas Medical Center, but the truth is some highly qualified doctor in a backwater town might like the idea of spending some time on an exotic island with easy access to Europe."

"Thank you," she said, her mind already exploring possibilities. "I hadn't thought of that."

Tina squeezed her husband's arm. "What an intelligent, resourceful man."

"Well, I got you, didn't I?" he said and Bridget felt a

twinge of longing. How would it feel if Ryder acted the same way toward her? Biting her lip, she gave herself a hard mental shake. She had other plans. Italy beckoned.

She arrived at the exclusive restaurant and was seated with Tina and Zach. Ryder arrived fifteen minutes later, appearing distracted as he strode to the table. "Sorry," he said and leaned down to kiss her full on the mouth. "I've missed the hell out of you," he whispered.

He turned to Tina and Zach. "Your Highness," he said. "Your Highness's husband."

Both Tina and Zach chuckled. "Please call me Tina," she said.

"And I'm Zach," he said, rising to offer his hand.

"Excuse me if I'm checking my cell phone messages. I have a patient teetering on the edge tonight. He's diabetic and I would have preferred not to operate, but this wasn't an optional procedure."

"Is this the same patient you were watching last night?" Bridget asked.

"Yes," Ryder said. "He improved, but I'm concerned about circulation to his extremities."

Bridget automatically extended her hand toward his beneath the table. Ryder responding by clasping it against his knee. "If you need to leave," she began.

"I can stay for now. I just need to check my messages," he said.

"We're glad you could join us," Tina said. "You've certainly captured Bridget's attention and that's not easy to do."

Bridget fought a rise of heat to her cheeks. "Tina," she said.

"Really?" Ryder said. "That's encouraging news

because wherever she goes the men are chasing after her."

"I told you that's just because of my title," Bridget said.

"Not true," he said.

"Exactly," Tina said, and Bridget felt her sister study her intently.

Bridget picked up the menu. "I wonder what the specials are tonight."

The waiter took their orders, Ryder frequently checked his phone messages and even excused himself once to make a call.

"Is this what you want for your future?" Tina asked. "He's been half-focused on his phone throughout the entire meal."

"He could have cancelled, but he came. If someone important to you was in the hospital, wouldn't you want to know his doctor was this conscientious?"

Tina frowned. "I suppose. I just can't see you being happy with someone so intent on his career."

Bridget leaned forward. "Ryder and I haven't made any mention of commitment," she whispered. "We're just enjoying each other's company."

"As long as he's not enjoying the company too much," Zach said.

"I'm not pregnant, if that's what you're asking," she said.

"Low blow," Tina said.

"You deserve it," Bridget said, feeling pushed to the edge. "Stefan told me you tattled about me seeing Ryder. I would have expected better from you."

"It's my duty to look after you," Tina said.

"Isn't that the same thing Stefan said to you?" Bridget challenged.

Tina gasped in offense. "Well—"

Ryder reappeared at the table, relief written on his face. "Good news. My patient's condition is improving."

"Excellent news," Bridget said as the waiter cleared the plates from the table.

"Excellent," Tina agreed, though she shot Bridget a sharp look. "Bridget tells me you've recently taken over the guardianship of twin baby boys. That must have been traumatic for all of you. My sympathies on the loss of your brother and sister-in-law."

"Thanks," Ryder said. "Bridget has actually helped smooth the waters with the twins. She found a nanny who has been a perfect fit. Until she stepped in, I was scrambling. I had several quit on me. With my profession, I need dependable childcare."

"Well done, Bridget," Tina said, appearing impressed and vaguely surprised.

"Your friend Keely helped. She gave me the name of the top nanny agency in Dallas," Bridget said.

"But Bridget interviewed the candidates and selected the final choice," he said.

"Bridget isn't known for her affinity for babies," Tina said.

Thanks for nothing, Bridget thought.

"Neither am I," Ryder said bluntly. "But she stepped right in. She's been a lifesaver. The boys adore her."

"And what about you?" Tina asked. "What are your intentions?"

"Tina," Bridget scolded.

"It's a good question," Zach said, backing up his wife.

Bridget balled her fists in her lap. "You do not have to answer that question, Ryder."

Ryder placed his hand over hers underneath the table. "I don't mind answering. Bridget and I have just met. Neither of us know what the future holds. Based on the demands our lives place on us, I know our relationship is temporary."

Bridget's heart fell to her feet. Even though she agreed with Ryder's assessment, hearing the words wounded her to the quick. *She was temporary.*

The interminable meal finally ended fifteen minutes later. Ryder shook hands with her sister and brother-in-law, then brushed a kiss against the corner of her mouth. "Miss you," he murmured just for her ears. "Call me."

A few moments later, she sat in the back of her brother-in-law's SUV, still feeling shell-shocked.

"I can see why you like him," Tina said. "He's his own man and clearly isn't after you because you're royalty. Plus, it doesn't appear that he intends to keep you from going to Italy," she added with a low laugh.

Bridget couldn't muster the careless response she should have been able to toss back to her sister. Silence stretched inside the car.

"Bridget, are you okay? Why are you so quiet?" Tina asked, turning around to look at her.

Bridget thanked heaven for the darkness. "I'm just tired," she said.

"Are you sure? You were always such a night owl."

"I'm sure," she said, trying not to resent her sister for pressing Ryder. It had been so much easier for her when her relationship with Ryder had remained undefined. Some part of her must have craved the sense of possibility with him. He was so different from any man she'd ever known. Ryder and the babies almost made her rethink Italy.

Blessedly, Zach pulled in front of her hotel. Relief rushed through her. If she could just get upstairs without another inquisition. "It was so wonderful seeing both of you. Thank you for dinner," she said and stepped outside the car when the valet opened her door.

Tina rushed outside her door. "Bridget," she said, studying her face. "I know something is wrong."

"Nothing is wrong," Bridget said, pushing a strand of her hair behind her ear. "I told you I'm just tired."

"I don't believe you," Tina said. "I can sense you're upset."

Bridget lost her patience. "Why should I be upset? You just grilled my boyfriend and me. I had a perfectly wonderful evening planned with him, but instead we went to dinner with you and might as well have been sent to walk across coals."

She watched her sister's face fall in desolation. "I'm so sorry," Tina said. "Zach and I just wanted to make sure this man wasn't going to take advantage of you."

"Would you have wanted Zach to receive the same kind of grilling you gave me?"

"I didn't know you felt the same way about Ryder that I felt about Zach," Tina said.

"It doesn't matter how you judge my feelings. It matters how I judge my feelings. I'm an adult. I don't need my sister, brother, brother-in-law and everyone else legislating or judging who I see." She lifted her chin. "Have a little faith in me for a change."

Tina's eyes turned shiny with tears. "Oh, I'm so

sorry. I did the same thing to you that I didn't want done to me."

Bridget took a quick sharp breath. She hated to hurt her sister, but Bridget needed Tina to believe in her. Just a little. "Yes, you did. Do you really believe I'm so stupid that any man can get my attention?" she asked, then continued before her sister could continue. "I know I acted like a spoiled brat when I had to come back from Italy after two weeks to cover for you, but I still came back and I still covered. I'm not a total ditz."

"Oh, Bridget," Tina said, shaking her head and clasping Bridget's hands. "I never thought you were a ditz. I always knew you were underestimated. I owe you a huge debt for stepping in for me and also dealing with Stefan. I just don't want you to be hurt."

Bridget bit the inside of her lip. Too late for that, she thought. "I won't be," she reassured her sister and gave her a hug.

"Don't be mad at me," Tina whispered.

"I'm not," Bridget said.

"Promise?" Tina asked.

"Promise," Bridget said.

"You'll never bring another man around me, will you?" Tina asked.

"It'll be a while," Bridget said with a rough laugh. "I need to hit the sack. Long day tomorrow. I love you." She waved to Zach and gave her sister one more hug, then walked inside the hotel toward her suite. When she got inside, she collapsed on her bed and gave in to her tears.

Bridget soldiered through her appointments the next day. Just after four-thirty as she was headed back to her hotel to change for a dinner appearance, she received a call from Suzanne.

"Your Highness, I probably shouldn't call you, but I thought you should know," the nanny said in a tear-filled voice.

"What is it? What's wrong?" Bridget asked.

"It's Travis. His fever shot up to 105 degrees," she said. "We had to take him to the hospital because it was too late for the pediatrician."

Bridget's heart sank to her feet. "Where is Ryder?"

"He's at the hospital," she said. "In the emergency room with a pediatric specialist." She gave a muffled sob. "I'm at Ryder's with Tyler."

She fought the urge to hyperventilate. Nothing could happen to that baby. Nothing. "I'm going to the hospital."

"Ryder didn't tell me to call you," Suzanne said.

"Well, he bloody well should have," Bridget said and told her driver to head for the hospital.

Ryder had never felt so helpless in his life as he watched his nephew, now his son, suffer the tests necessary to make him well. Travis screamed at the top of his lungs. "I'm sorry, Dr. McCall, but I think we're going to need to do a spinal tap."

Sweating everything but blood, Ryder nodded. "Do what you have to do to make him well." Ryder was well aware that Travis's condition was deteriorating. He couldn't remember feeling this kind of terror ever before.

After the spinal, Ryder heard a ruckus outside the examination room. A nurse entered. "I'm sorry, but there's a woman outside. She says she's a princess. She insists to be allowed inside with you and your son."

The nurse may as well have hit him with both fists. *She's a princess.* It was Bridget. A crazy sliver of relief slid through him. *Your son.* The words echoed inside his brain over and over. "Let her in," he said.

Seconds later, Bridget burst into the room wearing a hospital gown. She glanced from him to Travis, who was curled up exhausted on the table. Ryder would have preferred his cranky cries to his silence. He touched the baby's arm.

Bridget touched Ryder's.

Struggling with a terrible sense of desperation, he covered her hand with his.

"Can I hold him?" she asked.

"Not yet." They'd been instructed to wait to hold Travis, who was hooked up to an IV.

"He's going to be all right," she said softly as she held Ryder's hand. "He's a strong baby."

"He's always the one to cry the loudest and the longest," Ryder said, surprised at the strength of the fear he was fighting. Medically, he understood everything that was being done, but some part of him felt it wasn't enough. There had to be more. There had to be a way.

A few more moments passed. Bridget squeezed his hand and took a deep breath. "Can we hold him now?" she asked the nurse when she entered the room.

"For just a few moments," she said. "Take care for his IV."

Bridget sat and held Travis. His vital signs showed less stress within a moment of her cuddling him. Ryder took his turn holding the baby a while later and he was surprised to see he had the same effect on him.

Sometime later, the pediatrician strode into the room. "Lab results are back. Strep," he said. "With antibiotics, he'll be better in no time."

"Are you sure?" Bridget asked. "He seems so listless."

The pediatrician smiled gently. "With the right treatment, these little guys recover so quickly they make me look like a miracle worker. You just need to make sure everyone who's been exposed to him receives preventative treatment, too."

"Tyler," Bridget said to Ryder.

"And Suzanne and the other sitters. Thanks, Carl," he said to the pediatrician. "I know you stayed late for this. I owe you."

"I'm glad it was so easy," he said and glanced at Bridget. "And I don't believe I've met your wife."

Ryder felt a twist of awkwardness, but rushed to correct his colleague for Bridget's sake. "She's not my wife, but we've been damn lucky to have her around. This is Bridget Devereaux."

Carl nodded. "You clearly have a calming effect on the baby. You must be a natural."

Bridget laughed wryly. "I'm not sure I'd call myself a natural, but I'm relieved Travis will be okay. Thank you so very much."

"No problem. We'll have him stay the rest of the night. I wouldn't be surprised if he'll be ready to be released by midday. I'll talk to you later," he said and headed out the door.

Ryder stared at Bridget tenderly holding his nephew, his child, as if Travis were her own child. Something inside him shifted. Stone walls he'd long considered closed cracked open and he felt a burst of sweet oxygen in places that had felt dead. The expansion inside him was almost painful. For a second, he looked away to gather his defenses, to put himself back together the way he needed to be.

When he looked at her again, he saw a tear drop from her eye to Travis's gown. She gave a quick sound of distress and swiped at her cheek.

The sight of her tears shocked him. Bridget was no crybaby. "Are you okay?"

"I apologize," she said, not lifting her head. "I was just so frightened for him. And I felt so helpless."

He couldn't not reach out to her. Pushing her hair from her cheek, he felt the dampness of her tears against the back of his fingers. "Yeah," he said. "Me, too."

She finally met his gaze. "They're so fragile. One minute, he was screaming bloody murder and trying to scoot to get a ball, and the next…this," she said, looking down at Travis as he slept, his energy clearly spent fighting his infection.

Moved more than he'd thought possible, Ryder kissed her cheek. "Thank you for coming."

"There was no other place more important for me to be," she said and met his gaze again.

The powerful emotion he saw in her gaze resonated inside him so strongly that it took his breath. What the hell was going on? Later, he told himself. He would figure it out later. For the moment, his priorities were perfectly clear. Travis and Bridget.

Just as Carl predicted, within hours, Travis began to make a miraculous recovery. He downed a bottle and afterward seemed to be looking for the rest of the meal. "They told us to go slow on the solids," Bridget said as she fed the baby some applesauce.

"But he looks like he's wanting a steak dinner," Ryder said, pleased with Travis's improvement.

Bridget laughed. "I agree, but he won't be getting that from me."

"He won't be getting that from anyone, no matter how cranky he gets," Ryder said protectively.

Moments later, Carl dropped by, examined the baby and released him. Bridget wanted to ride home with him and the baby. As they walked out of the hospital in the hot summer sun, two men with cameras and microphones suddenly swarmed them.

"Princess Bridget, you've been spending a lot of time with Dr. Ryder McCall and his nephews. Are the two of you serious or is this just a fling?" the reporter asked.

Anger rushed through Ryder, and he stepped in front of her before she could respond. "It's none of your business. Leave her alone. Can't you see we're bringing a recovering baby home from the hospital?"

"But the people want to know," the reporter continued.

"The people don't need to know. It's none of their business," Ryder said.

"You obviously don't understand that royals belong to their people," the man said and tried to shove Ryder aside to get to Bridget.

"Leave her alone," Ryder said and knocked the man to the ground.

A half second later, Bridget's security guard swept her and the baby into a limo.

"But, Ryder," Bridget protested as her guard closed the door of the limo.

The reporter on the ground winced in pain at the same time he shouted to the cameraman, "Did you catch all that? It'll be worth a fortune."

Chapter Ten

"You must leave Dr. McCall's house this instant," Stefan said to Bridget over the phone.

Bridget rolled her eyes. "I'm not going to do that. We just brought Travis home. He still needs comfort and Ryder can't do it all."

"Bridget, you're not the mother of these children. You have other duties, and now that the paparazzi has found you, Dr. McCall's house will be stalked day and night. For your safety, let alone your reputation, you can't stay there."

"Oh, to hell with my reputation. If I'm going to be crucified by the press, I can't think of a better reason."

"You're not thinking rationally," Stefan said. "Perhaps I should pull you from this assignment for your own good."

Bridget's heart froze. "You wouldn't dare," she said.

"Of course I would dare," he said. "I must make the calls for everyone's best interest."

"Give me two weeks," she said, determined to keep the desperation out of her voice. "You owe me that."

Silence followed. "It's true that Phillipa will be coming soon, but your doctor friend will need to be prepared for extra security at his house," Stefan said. "I get the impression he doesn't like a lot of intrusion in his private life. He may not like being told what to do."

"Of course he won't," she said. "Would you?"

"That's different," Stefan said.

"He won't what?" Ryder asked from the doorway, his shirt clinging to him in perspiration.

Her heart jumped and she covered the receiver. "It's my brother. He's being impossible."

"I'm not being impossible," Stefan said. "Let me talk to the doctor."

"Let me talk to your brother," Ryder said.

Bridget cringed. "I'd really rather the two of you meet in different circumstances."

"Sorry, sweetheart," Ryder said.

"Now is the time," Stefan said.

Bridget reluctantly handed the phone to Ryder. "Just start out with Your Highness," she whispered.

Ryder took the phone. "Good to meet you, Your Highness," Ryder said. "Your sister has been a godsend to my family."

Silence followed and Ryder tilted his head to one side.

"My position as adviser to the residents at my hospital can't be influenced by my feelings for your sister,"

Ryder said. "I can't send doctors to Chantaine if it's not in their best interest."

Bridget heard Stefan's raised voice and turned her head, wincing.

"I'm sure you understand my responsibility," Ryder said. "Just as you must make the best decisions for your country, I must make the best decisions in advising my residents."

Another quick silence followed, and Ryder met her gaze. "I have no objection to having additional security so that Bridget can come and go here as she pleases. I don't want what happened today to happen again."

A moment later, he said, "We agree on more than you think. Maybe we'll meet in person sometime. Bye for now, Your Highness."

He turned off the phone and handed it to her. "Your brother is a tough negotiator. Not as charming as you," he added with a low laugh. "And I'm sure he's not as hot."

She bit her lip, but couldn't keep from smiling. She closed her eyes for a second, then opened them. "I can be a lot of trouble. My family can be a lot of trouble."

He shrugged. "Everything can be trouble. Depends on whether it's worth it. Come back in the den. Travis is calling for you."

Bridget stayed the day and the day turned to evening. Ryder gave the okay for additional security around the house. He asked Raoul to keep it as invisible as possible. Raoul agreed. Ryder found he couldn't dislike Bridget's guard because he felt the same need to protect her. He was still trying to remember the time he'd punched someone in defense of a woman….

And he would damn well do it again and again for Bridget....

When those reporters had rushed him and Bridget, he'd acted instinctively, with a primitive response. They'd gotten way too close for comfort to Bridget and his baby. His head was still swimming with the reality.

Ryder hadn't realized how important Bridget and the babies had become to him. It was turning him inside out.

That night, against Raoul's advice, she stayed the night. Ryder took her to his bed and stripped off her clothes. He kissed every inch of her, then took her with every beat of his heart and every beat of hers.

His gaze wrapped around hers. At the same time that he took her, Ryder felt taken. In a way he'd never felt before.

Bridget clung to Ryder as he tried to rise from the bed in the morning. He gave a low chuckle that rippled through her.

"Don't want me to leave?"

"I don't," she said, sliding her hands over his muscular chest. "Pippa is coming to Dallas."

"Pippa?" he echoed, scouring her gaze.

"My sister Phillipa," she said. "She's having some problems. I'll have to entertain her a bit. You and I may not have as much time to be together."

"What kind of problems?" he asked, leaning down on his left forearm.

"I'm not sure, but she's stressed enough that my brother sent her here to visit Valentina and me."

He gave a slow nod. "You have a complicated family."

Her heart twisted. "I warned you."

He nodded. "So you did. When do I see you again?"

"I'll have to call you. I'm not sure when she arrives in the States."

"Call me today. I have surgery, but I'll check my messages in between."

Bridget scrambled to make her appointments for the day, then met Ryder at home that night. In between cuddling the twins, they ate sandwiches prepared by Suzanne and Ryder's friend Marshall.

"They seem to be growing very cozy," she said to Ryder as they leaned back against the sofa with the TV playing a ball game about which neither cared.

"Who?" Ryder asked, sliding his hand around hers.

"Suzanne and Marshall," she said.

Ryder groaned. "Don't tell me that. Marshall doesn't have a good history with women. His maximum time is weeks, not months. Days are more likely."

She shrugged. "You never know. Maybe she's the one. Maybe he's ready for the real thing and he's decided she's the real thing."

She felt him study her. "What do you think about the real thing?"

"I think the real thing starts on its own and then you have to keep it going," she said, but when she looked at him, she felt herself spin with emotion. "What about you?"

"I don't know. I always thought it was a figment of everyone's imagination," he said.

"And now?"

He shrugged his muscular shoulders. "Now, I'm not so sure."

Bridget hit the campaign trail for doctors for Chantaine hard. As one of her last resorts, she even met with the administrator of another medical hospital in Dallas. They were more open to her proposal of sending doctors to her country.

Bridget felt torn at the prospect. She wanted only the best for her country, but she couldn't automatically turn down the hospital's interest. It was more than Ryder could offer. The knowledge stabbed at her. She hated that he couldn't feel her passion for her country the same way she did.

In the meantime, she took deep breaths and decided not to make any impulsive decisions. That night, after rocking the babies, she joined Ryder in his bed. He made love to her with a passion that took her breath away.

Ryder drew her into his arms, flush against his body. She felt his heart beat against her chest. She had never felt closer to another human being in her life.

Travis recovered quickly. It seemed that one moment the baby had been listless and the next he was raring to go, trying to pull up and almost scooting, heaven help them all.

Phillipa arrived at DFW and Bridget greeted her sister with open arms. Bridget was concerned to see that Phillipa had indeed lost weight and there were circles beneath her eyes. "Hello, my darling," Bridget said. "I'm so glad to see you."

Phillipa slumped against her for a moment. "It's so good to see you, too," she murmured, squeezing Bridget tightly.

Bridget's concern deepened, but her instincts told her to mask it. At least for now. "I must prepare you for the Texas humidity," she said. "You can cut the air with a knife. We're headed to Tina's ranch. I'm sure she'll be calling any minute. She's dying to see you." Seconds later, her cell phone rang. "Just as I said." She picked up. "Yes, Tina, she's here and as soon as we get her luggage, we're headed straight for your house."

Bridget nodded and smiled. "Soon, soon. Ciao for now."

She hustled Pippa into the limo, plied her with a couple margaritas, and chattered during the drive to Tina's about Texas and the twins and Ryder. "Of course, Stefan is complaining," she said. "I swear he'd like to put us all in convents."

"So true," Phillipa said. "How did you deal with him?"

Bridget made a mental note of Phillipa's comment. Was Phillipa's problem romance? "Avoidance is the best policy," she said. "Emails. Text messages. Direct conversation is the worst because Stefan is disgustingly intuitive. If he would only get Eve pregnant, maybe he would be a bit distracted."

Phillipa chuckled. "Eve doesn't want to rush another child. She wants to give Stephenia plenty of time to adjust."

"Blast her practicality," Bridget said and took her second sip of her first margarita. "Well, you should know that Tina will arrange for massages and spa treatments.

Zach may take us out on his fabulous boat. We also have a social ball to attend in four days."

"Social ball," Phillipa echoed, clearly concerned.

"Oh, it's nothing to worry about," Bridget soothed. "It's a charity gala in Dallas. Tina and Zach will attend. If you like, we can make an appearance and bug out. You know I'm quick like that when it suits me. Stefan has fussed about it enough. Plus we can go shopping before and you can get a great dress out of it."

Pippa gave a mild smile. "So we don't have to stay all night?"

"Of course not," Bridget said, patting her sister on her knee. "Have the doctoral studies become a pain in the butt? You know, you work entirely too hard."

"My studies are fine, but Stefan insisted I take a break," she said.

"He means well," Bridget said. "But he still needs some work. I'm hopeful Eve can continue his needed transformation."

Phillipa sighed and took another sip of her margarita. "Bridget, you have no idea how much I've needed to see you."

Still concerned, Bridget managed a laugh. "Well, prepare yourself for an overdose."

Pippa smiled and Bridget felt as if she'd scored a small victory. Later, as they arrived at the ranch, Tina rushed down the steps. "Phillipa!" she called stretching out her arms.

Bridget watched her two sisters embrace and her heart squeezed tight with emotion. Tina pulled back. "Look at you. I love your hair. That dress is fabulous. What happened to my sister, the librarian?"

"I'm still here," Phillipa said. "A stylist put together some things for my visit to the States."

"Regardless, you look fabulous, but shorts and no shoes are the summertime uniform here. Come visit your niece. She can't wait to see Aunt Pippa," Tina said, and tossed Bridget a glance of concern before she led them inside the house.

Bridget and Phillipa played with their gorgeous niece until dinnertime when Hildie served a superb, filling meal. Between the margaritas, the food and the security of her sisters, Phillipa grew drowsy early in the evening. Tina ushered her to one of the bedrooms and returned to the den with Bridget and Zach.

"She's different than I expected," Tina said. "Stefan said she was stressed, but—" Tina frowned. "What do you think is behind all this?"

"A man," Bridget said as she sipped a glass of ice water.

Tina's eyebrows rose. "What makes you say that?"

"Something Pippa said on the way here."

"What? Who?" Tina demanded.

"I didn't pry. She just seemed too fragile," Bridget said.

Tina sighed. "How did you get that out of her?"

"It was a sideways comment. I was complaining about Stefan and how he doesn't want any of us to date."

"True," Tina said.

"Too true," Zach said from behind the newspaper he was reading.

Tina glanced at her husband and smiled.

"In this case, I was speaking of Ryder," Bridget said.

"Hmm," Tina said.

"So far, he seems like a good guy," Zach said. "If he was willing to punch out that reporter who was after you, he gets my vote."

"It's all about the violence," Tina said, rolling her eyes.

"Protecting a woman is a primitive response in a man. Protectiveness is an important trait."

"I'm sure Stefan will love hearing that opinion," Bridget said wryly.

"Stefan just needs to be reminded about what he would do to protect Eve," Zach said bluntly, then shook his newspaper and appeared to begin to read again.

"She needs a massage," Tina said. "A ride on the water. And perhaps Hildie's double-strength margaritas."

Three days later, the sisters went to Dallas and shopped for dresses. Bridget was distracted. She was late. Not for an appointment. She was late for her period, and she had been, well, exposed to the possibility of becoming pregnant. Although they had used contraception, Bridget wasn't sure if she had landed in the small percentile of women for whom it had failed.

"What do you think?" Tina asked as Phillipa tried on a gown. "I think the cocoa color is perfect on her."

Bridget blinked, looking at Pippa. "Yes, it's beautiful. It really accentuates all your positive attributes."

"Although, a pastel or dark navy would be fabulous, too, don't you think?" Tina said.

"I completely agree," she said and forced herself to pay attention to the rest of the shopping expedition. She rendered her positive opinion to Tina's choice for a dress, but nixed the idea of getting a new gown for herself.

Tina and Phillipa gasped at once. "Are you ill?" Phillipa asked.

"What is wrong?" Tina demanded. "You never turn down the opportunity to get a new designer gown."

Bridget brushed their concerns aside. "It's nothing," she said. "I have a ton of gowns I brought with me that I haven't yet worn. We've already spent enough time shopping. It's not necessary to find a gown for me."

"Enough time shopping," Pippa echoed. "You've often said there's no such thing as too much shopping."

Uncomfortable with her sisters' scrutiny, Bridget shrugged her shoulders. "Okay, I'll admit it. I'm hungry and we might end up with rubber chicken tonight."

Tina giggled and rolled her eyes. "Now we have the real answer. I could use a good meal, too. Crab sounds especially good."

The thought of crab turned Bridget's stomach. "Or even a nice sandwich. You know where we can find a good variety of food, Tina. Where should we go?"

Delighted to give the attention back to her sister, Bridget joined her sisters for a late lunch. Her phone rang during their meal and she excused herself to take the call. "Ryder, talk to me. I swear it feels as if it's been three months since I heard your voice."

He laughed. "Same here. Are you having fun with your sisters?"

"For the most part," she said. "We still haven't figured out what's wrong with Phillipa, but I think it's a man. I'm hoping she'll talk with us. It's always more miserable to suffer by yourself. And whatever your problems are, they seem ten times worse if you don't share. Speaking of worries, how are you and the twins?"

"The only way the twins and I could be better would be if you were around," he said.

Her heart went squishy at his words. "Oh, that's so sweet. They've probably already forgotten me."

"No chance."

"You know, the other day, I was wondering, did you ever think you were going to have children? I know becoming a doctor was important, but did you *ever* think you would start a family?"

"It wasn't a priority," he said. "My career was always number one.... Just a moment," he said and she heard him talking with someone else. Then he came back on the line. "Listen, I need to go soon. Are you okay? I'm hearing something in your voice."

"Oh, no," she said, lying because she knew she didn't have time to discuss her real feelings. "It's just family stuff."

He paused a few seconds. "But you mentioned starting a family. What's on your mind?"

"Nothing," she insisted. "I was just thinking about how you'd been thrust into the position of being a father so quickly. I wondered what your original plans were."

She heard him give a quick response to someone on the other end of the line. "Are you pregnant?"

Shocked at the accuracy of his question, she sucked in a quick breath. Something inside her insisted on denial. She would figure that out later. "Oh, my goodness. How could I be pregnant? You and I are so careful."

"Nothing provides perfect protection except abstinence," he said.

"Oh, that's ridiculous. We're fine. We're perfectly fine," she insisted, her heart racing.

"Thanks for the reassurance," he said. "You and I both have enough going on without adding a baby to the mix."

"So true," she said, but her stomach twisted viciously.

"I have to go. I'll call later."

"Ciao," she said and stared blindly at her cell phone. What if she *was* pregnant? It was clear that Ryder didn't want another baby. How would she handle this? Would she have to do it all alone? Panic raced through her. She broke into a cold sweat. She shuddered at the possibility of dealing with her family's disapproval and interference.

"Bridget," her sister Tina said, breaking her out of her reverie. "The food's been here for several minutes. What's wrong with you today? You seem totally distracted."

Bridget took a breath and pulled herself together, forcing a big smile. "Oh, Tina, you know how I am. If I've got more than one and a half things on my mind, I'm distracted. I'm still thinking about the babies and the medical program for Chantaine. I need that sandwich. Thank you for coming to get me," she said and marched back to the table, praying her sister wouldn't ask any more questions.

That night, Bridget and her sisters dressed at her suite at the hotel. She felt as if she were on automatic. A green dress. Green was a good color for her. Mineral powder, subtle eyes, bold, red lips. She didn't feel bold, but she needed to be confident. She needed to be someone bigger than her current self because her current self was feeling confused and vulnerable. Lord, she hoped it was late PMS.

She gave her sister Phillipa a hug. "You look fabulous."

"You overstate," Phillipa said. "You always have."

"Not this time. Look at how gorgeous you look," she said, pointing to the full-length mirror.

Tina stepped into the room from the bathroom. "What are you two arguing about?"

"I told Phillipa she looked fabulous and gorgeous and she said I'm exaggerating and I said I'm not," Bridget said.

Tina walked to Phillipa and put her hands tenderly on her cheeks. "For once, Bridget understated."

Phillipa closed her eyes and squeezed them tight as if she were fighting tears. "You two are being so kind. I know all of this is because you're worried about me."

"Well, it's true we're worried about you," Bridget said.

"Bridget," Tina said with a chiding expression.

"It's true. It's also true that I wouldn't include fabulous and gorgeous in the same sentence if I didn't truly believe it," Bridget said.

Phillipa's lips twitched. "You make a good point. The real you leaks out after a short time."

Bridget lifted her hand. "What did I say?"

Tina sighed. "We just want you to be okay. You're our baby," she said, stroking Phillipa's hair.

"I'm not a baby. I'm a grown-up. I can manage my life. I just need a little recalibration."

"And you can get that here," Tina said.

Phillipa smiled. Tina's cell phone rang and she picked up. "It's Zachary."

Moments later, Zachary arrived in a limo driven by security. The three princesses and Zach rode to the charity ball. As they stepped outside the limo, they were greeted by flashing cameras and reporters.

"Welcome to Dallas's premier Charity Ball, Your Highnesses. To what do we owe the honor of your presence tonight?" a reporter asked.

Just lucky, I guess, Bridget thought, but managed to swallow the comment.

"I live just outside of Fort Worth with my husband and daughter, and I've been so happy to receive visits from both my sisters, Bridget and Phillipa," Tina said.

"Your sister Bridget has been in town for over a month. There have been rumors about her and one of our doctors—"

"We're here tonight to celebrate the charity of the people of Texas, which is so much bigger than rumors, don't you agree?" Tina asked. "It was lovely to meet you."

They moved on to the next reporter, and Tina's responses reminded Bridget why her sister had done such a superlative job representing Chantaine.

"She's so good," Bridget muttered.

"Times two," Phillipa said.

"If only she could be in two places at once," Bridget said with a sigh.

"You're doing pretty well," Pippa said.

"My time is limited," Bridget said. "I don't have Tina's endurance."

"Maybe, this once, you underestimate yourself," her sister said.

"I think not, but I appreciate your kindness. On to our rubber chicken," she whispered and was thrilled she could make Phillipa laugh.

"What are you two talking about?" Tina demanded.

"You don't want to know," Bridget said.

Tina shot her a curt micro-look before she plastered a serene expression on her face. Zach escorted the group inside to their table at the front of the room. They made small talk with the others seated at their table. Soon enough, announcements and presentations began. Bridget was stunned when Nic LaFitte stepped forward to receive an award of recognition. The Devereaux had a long-standing grudge against the Lafittes. Nic's father had caused a humiliating scandal for the royal family.

"What is *he* doing here?" she whispered to Tina.

"Zach says he's a huge contributor here. Everyone loves him," Tina said distastefully.

"They clearly don't know him," she said and nudged Phillipa. "Why can't we escape him?" she whispered. "Maybe it's because he's the devil and that means he can be everywhere."

When Phillipa didn't respond, Bridget glanced at her face and saw that her sister had turned white as a sheet.

Chapter Eleven

"I'm not feeling well," Phillipa said. "Please excuse me."

"Do you want me to go with you?" Bridget asked, her stomach twisting in concern for her sister.

"No, no. I just need a little air," Phillipa said as she slowly rose and lifted her lips in a forced smile. "I'll be back in a little bit."

Bridget watched her sister move through the perimeter of the room as surreptitiously as possible and felt worried.

"Where is she going?" Tina asked in a whisper.

"The powder room," Bridget said. "She says she needs some air."

Tina frowned and glanced at Nic LaFitte as he left the stage. "Do you think this has anything to do with LaFitte?"

"I can't imagine that it would. I mean, none of us

would get involved with a LaFitte. Not even the most rebellious of us and Pippa is nowhere near the most rebellious."

Tina nodded and Bridget paid half attention to the speaker, more attention to her watch. "I'm going to check on Pippa," she whispered.

"I'll go with you," Tina said, and stood just after she did.

Bridget tried to be discreet just as Phillipa had been, but she noticed several heads turning in her direction. She immediately searched for the first ladies' room and didn't find Phillipa there. "Where is she?" she muttered to herself.

"I'm starting to get a bad feeling about LaFitte," Tina said as they left the room.

"I can't believe Pippa would be that foolish. She's extremely intelligent and quite practical," Bridget said as she scoured the lobby for her sister.

"I wonder if she went outside," Tina said.

"It's possible. She said she needed some air," Bridget said, then spotted a coat closet and pointed toward it. "You don't think she would be there, do you? It's the last place I would look in this hot, humid weather and the door is closed."

Tina glanced in the same direction and shrugged. "I don't think so, but we may as well check."

Bridget led the way to the door and stopped just outside, pressing her ear closer to listen. Hearing nothing, she cracked the door open.

"This is insanity," Phillipa said. "It will never work."

"Why not?" a male voice demanded. "If I want you and you want me, what is most important?"

"Want is a temporary emotion," Phillipa said. "There are more important things than temporary emotions."

"If that's true, then why are you here with me?" he asked.

Tina gasped and the sound traveled through the door like a thunderclap. Seconds later, Phillipa and Nic LaFitte appeared in the doorway.

"Get away from my sister," Bridget said.

"That's for her to say, not you," LaFitte said.

"You're just using her," Tina said. "You only want her because she can redeem your terrible family name."

"Not everyone finds my family name reprehensible. Some even respect it," he said.

"That's respect you've bought with money," Tina said. "Leave Phillipa alone. You can never be good enough for her. If you have any compassion, you'll at least protect her reputation by leaving now."

LaFitte tightened his jaw. "I'll leave, but Phillipa will make the ultimate decision about the future of our relationship." He glanced behind him and met Phillipa's shocked, pale face. "Ciao, darling. Call me when you get some courage. Some things are meant to be," he said and strode away.

"Oh, darling," Bridget said and immediately went to Phillipa and took her in her arms.

Tina soon followed. "Oh, you poor thing. The LaFittes are so evil. It's clear he intends to trick you."

Phillipa's face crumpled. "He was so kind to me," she whispered.

"Of course he was," Tina said. "He's a snake like the rest of his family. And you're too sweet to know the difference."

"Are you saying he couldn't possibly be attracted to me just because I'm me?" Phillipa asked, her voice filled with desperation.

Bridget felt her heart shatter at the pain in her sister's voice. "Of course not," she said. "You're an amazing, beautiful and wonderful girl. You're a precious gem and you must be protected from anyone who doesn't deserve you."

"And no LaFitte would *ever* deserve you," Tina said.

Moments later, out of consideration for Phillipa, they left the event. Bridget and Tina fought over where Phillipa should spend the night. Bridget eventually won. "She shouldn't have to ride an extra hour back to the ranch tonight," Bridget said. "I have plenty of room in my suite. Along with the makings of margaritas or any other toddy she may require tonight."

"But Zach and I could protect her from any unwanted advances from LaFitte," Tina said.

"His advances weren't unwanted," Phillipa whispered. "I was attracted to him and wished he would contact me. I finally gave in and sent a message to him. He met me and that was how it all started."

Tina sucked in a sharp breath, then silence fell in the limousine. Zach tipped back a glass of bourbon.

"Well, I'm glad you came to your senses," Tina said.

Bridget gave Phillipa a hug. "We don't need to talk or think about this anymore tonight. You've already had enough stress tonight. You're due some rest. You can come to my room and fall asleep all snug and safe in your bed. You can think about LaFitte tomorrow if necessary. Tonight it's not necessary."

"You sound like that Scarlett O'Hara in the American film *Gone with the Wind*," Tina said.

"In this case, she offered a nice bit of wisdom," Bridget countered.

"Please don't argue," Phillipa said.

"We're not," Bridget said, giving Tina a strong glance. "Tina and I agree, don't we?"

Tina took a quick breath. "Yes, we do. I think we all need some extra rest tonight. In fact, I think Zach and I will stay overnight at your hotel."

"What?" Zach asked.

"Yes," Tina said decisively. "We can stay overnight at Bridget's hotel in a separate suite, of course. I'm sure Hildie won't mind keeping the baby."

"Yes, but—"

"In the morning, we can wake up and all have brunch together," she said brightly.

"And if Phillipa sleeps in, then Mom and Dad can enjoy a night away from their little darling and Phillipa can visit you at the ranch later."

Tina frowned, but nodded.

Moments later, they exited the limo into the hotel and Bridget and Phillipa took the lift to the penthouse. "Thank you," Phillipa said after they entered the elevator.

Bridget took her sister's hand. "We all need a break every now and then. If your sister won't give it to you, then who *will* give it to you?"

"Yes, but Tina clearly hates Nic," Bridget said in a shaky voice.

"All of us hate the LaFitte family. Part of it is not

logical. After all, if Father had married the woman who married LaFitte, none of us would exist. Maybe we don't like to lose. Plus there's the matter of the LaFitte who killed one of our great-uncles." Bridget sighed. "And, after all the bad they did to us, they're so bloody wealthy and successful. That's enough of a reason to hate them."

"His mother is dying," Phillipa said.

Bridget glanced at her sister. "Really. How?"

"Cancer. It's been a terribly grueling experience. She's currently near the end."

Bridget took a deep breath. "I don't wish that on anyone."

"Neither do I," Phillipa said as the elevator dinged their arrival to the penthouse.

Bridget clasped her sister's hand. "You must promise me that you won't think about this anymore tonight. You need to take a break from it. It's hurting you. More important, you can't fix it tonight."

Phillipa squeezed her hand in return. "I may not agree with a lot of what you've said, but it's true that I can't fix all of this tonight. I should just go to bed and try to sleep."

Bridget nodded. "And get a massage in the morning. I'll keep Tina away."

"You're usually nagging me to take on more palace duties. When did you become my fairy protector?" Phillipa asked.

"Oh, well, I'll nag again soon enough. Enjoy the respite," Bridget said.

The next morning, Bridget did just as she'd promised and arranged for a soothing massage for her younger sister. Tina would only be put off so long before she was knocking on the door of Bridget's suite. Bridget opened the door. "We're sipping lime water and relaxing on the balcony. Would you like to join us?" she asked. "And whatever you do, don't hound her and don't bring up LaFitte. I've got her nice and relaxed after her massage."

Tina nodded in agreement. "We'll take her out on Zach's new boat."

"But don't try to matchmake," Bridget said.

Tina frowned. "You don't think a male distraction would help?" she whispered.

"No," Bridget said emphatically. "Pippa has fallen hard for LaFitte. She needs to get over him before she moves on to the next."

"You seem to have enormous insight on this matter. Surprising," Tina said, lifting her eyebrow in a suspicious manner.

Bridget feigned an airy sigh. "Underestimated again. When will it end?"

After her sisters left, Bridget returned several calls. As soon as she finished, though, the quiet settled over her like a heavy blanket. She still hadn't started her period yet. Tempted to wear a disguise and buy an early pregnancy test from a drugstore, she put it off. She never knew who was watching and who might discuss her purchase with the paparazzi. Perhaps by tomorrow…

Her cell phone rang and she saw Ryder's return number on her screen. He was the one person to whom she hadn't made a return call. Her heart hammered with nerves as she took the call. "Hello, Ryder," she said.

"Damn good to hear your voice. I was starting to

wonder if you'd disappeared or headed to Chantaine or Italy without letting me know," he said.

"I wouldn't do that," she said. "I've just been tied up with my sisters. How are my boys?"

"Your boys are screaming to see you. Even Suzanne says they miss you. Come over for the weekend," he said.

Her heart jumped again and she began to pace. On the one hand, she was desperate to see Ryder again. On the other hand, she was distracted by the possibility that she could be pregnant. Ryder had been much more intuitive about her worries than she would have ever expected.

He made a buzzing sound. "Time's up. Because you didn't say no, that must mean yes. I'll pick you up around five," he said.

"Wait," she said breathlessly. "Let Raoul bring me. That way he can go through his security protocol and I won't be hassled by him or my brother. Hopefully," she added in a low voice.

"Good," Ryder said. "The twins have a trick they want to show you. See you soon," he said.

"Trick?" she echoed, but he'd already disconnected the call.

Anticipation zinged through her and she giggled. Her mood felt as if it had lifted into the stratosphere. Amazing that he had that effect on her so quickly. Frightening, really, if she thought about it too deeply, so she wouldn't.

A few hours later, she tried to ignore the lecture Raoul was giving her about how she was taking risks and how she should stay away from windows.

"Your Highness, do you understand what I'm saying?" Raoul asked.

"Absolutely," she said.

"You haven't been listening to a word I've said," he said.

"That's not true. I've listened to at least every third word you've said. I'm not reckless, but I won't let my position steal my joy. You never know how long you'll have that opportunity. There's so much drudgery you have to grab the joy."

Silence followed. "That's remarkably deep, Your Highness," he said. "But after protecting you for five years, I'm not surprised. You hide your depth well," he said, glancing at her through the rearview mirror.

Bridget felt a twist in her chest at her guard's revelation. "Thank you, Raoul. You deserve sainthood for being my guard."

"You are not as bad as you profess," he said. "But stay away from windows and call me before you walk outside the house."

She laughed as he pulled the car to the curb of Ryder's home. "Way to slide in those instructions," she said and opened her door before he could. "Ciao."

Before she arrived on the porch, the door flung open and Ryder greeted her, sweeping her inside. "Your men are waiting for you," he said and pulled her into his arms.

He felt so strong and wonderful and alive. She felt as if she'd come home. She was safe and more whole than she'd ever dreamed possible. He picked her up and spun her around and she couldn't help laughing.

"You act like you haven't seen me in a year," she said, squeezing his strong shoulders.

"It has been a year," he said and searched her face. "Right?"

A shriek sounded just a few steps away.

Bridget glanced at the floor and saw the twins scooting toward her and Ryder. "Oh, bloody hell," she said, panicked. "They're moving! We have to stop them."

Ryder roared with laughter. "That was my first response, too," he said and squeezed her shoulders. "But crawling is next. After that, standing. Then walking."

Bridget stared, torn between exultation and cold fear, and shook her head. "What are you going to do?"

"Cope," he said. "Manage them, if such a thing is possible. The good news is they get worn out a lot faster," he said.

Tyler stopped at Bridget's feet and gurgled.

Her heart twisted so tightly that she could hardly breathe. "Oh, you darling," she said and bent down to pick up the baby. She groaned. "You've gained weight. Is that possible?"

Ryder picked up Travis and extended him toward Bridget. She gave the baby a kiss and cooed at him. He cooed at her in return and her chest expanded, filling her with an overwhelming sense of love and emotion. "Oh, you darlings. I've missed both of you."

"Both?" Ryder asked.

"All three. Especially you," she said and sank onto the sofa with the baby on her lap. "The last few days have been full of drama. Poor Phillipa has been seduced by one of our family enemies. She's such an innocent. I know he's taken advantage of her, but I'm hoping she'll regain her sense."

"Who's this enemy? I thought you Devereaux were peaceful and moderate," he said, joining her on the sofa.

"We are for the most part," she said. "But the LaFittes have been bad news for our family. One of them murdered my great-uncle. And one seduced my father's bride away from him," she said.

"I can understand the first, but the second, not so much. You wouldn't have been born if your father had married a different woman," he said.

"True," she said. "But the LaFittes are still on our don't list. No discussion," she said.

"What about me?" he asked in a rough voice. "Am I on your don't list?"

Her breath hitched in the back of her throat. "Probably, but that hasn't stopped me, has it?"

His lips lifted in a lazy half grin. "Guess not. I ordered Italian for dinner. Bought red wine on the way home."

"Sounds great, but I'm all about water these days. I'm on a new diet that favors lemon and lime water. It's supposed to cleanse the toxins. Do you have any limes?"

Ryder blinked. "Limes?"

"No problem. Filtered water is good."

"So, red wine is out?" he asked.

"Just during my lime phase," she said with a smile.

They watched the twins scoot around the den until they wore themselves out. Ryder rocked Tyler and she rocked Travis. It took only moments before Travis was drooling on her shoulder. She met Ryder's gaze and he gave a slight nod and they carried the babies up to their cribs.

Seconds later, they walked downstairs and shared a

late meal. Although Italian fare didn't appeal to her at the moment, Bridget pushed the food around her plate to make it look as if she'd eaten it. Later, she took her plate into the kitchen and pushed the contents into the trash can.

Did this mean she was pregnant? she wondered. She loved Italian food. If she hated it, now what did it mean? Her stomach twisted into a knot, but she took a deep breath and returned to the den. "Delicious dinner," she said and sat down beside him.

"You didn't eat everything. It must not have been that delicious," he said, sliding his arm over her shoulder.

"I had a late lunch and I'm watching my girlish figure," she said with a smile.

"I'll take care of that second job. I have no problem watching your girlish figure," he said, sliding his lips along her neck.

She laughed, exulting in his caress. Turning toward him, she lifted her mouth to his. "Kiss me," she said.

"Is that an order?"

"Kinda," she said.

He gave a low, dirty chuckle and did as she commanded.

The next morning, Ryder awakened early. Bridget's back was pressed against him. His hand was curled around her bare waist. Her skin was butter soft against his palm. It was a good morning. The best kind of morning. Bridget was with him.

He couldn't remember a time when he'd been more at peace. Something primitive inside him drove him to keep her with him. He started to understand why men kidnapped their women and kept them in luxurious captivity. Which was crazy. When had he ever felt this need for a woman? When had a woman ever filled up all his emptiness and need?

Bridget wiggled against him, then suddenly raced out of bed to the master bath. A couple moments later, she returned, carefully crawling into the bed and inching herself toward him.

Several things clicked through his brain. His gut twisted. "Bridget," he murmured against her ear.

"Yes," she whispered.

"Are you pregnant?"

Silence passed. Way too long. His heart sank. *Another baby?* He couldn't imagine it. How in the world—

"I don't know," she finally said. "I'm late."

A half dozen emotions sliced through him. He couldn't speak.

"How late?" he finally managed.

"A week and a half," she said, still not turning to look at him.

"We should do a test," he said.

"No," she said. "I can't take a test, and you can't do it for me. The press is watching me even more than usual now. I want to know as much as you do, but a few more days may give us the answer without any exposure to the press," she said and finally turned toward him.

"You're late. No red wine. Why didn't you tell me?"

Her eyes clouded with turmoil. "Our relationship is still new. We haven't made any sort of promises to each other."

His heart pounded against his chest. The thought of another baby scared the crap out of him. His brother's babies had become his own. The baby he shared with Bridget would be his to protect as well.

"If you're pregnant, you need to start taking prenatal vitamins as soon as possible. You need to get on a regimen—"

"And if I'm not, I can go back to my red wine–swilling, unhealthy ways," she said.

He bit the inside of his lip to keep from laughing. "I still think you should let me do a test."

She shook her head. "Three more days. I'll live healthy until then."

He searched her face. "I would protect you if you're pregnant with my child, Bridget. I would marry you. I would protect our child."

Her eyes still swam with emotion, some of which he couldn't read. "That's good to know," she said and tucked her head under his chin. "Can we talk about something else until then?"

Ryder spent the weekend secluded in happiness with Bridget. They shared the care of the twins, took the boys for a stroll in the neighborhood despite Raoul's protests and spent their nights together, his body wrapped around hers, her body wrapped around his.

He returned to work Monday wondering if she was pregnant, wishing he could keep her with him. He met with Dr. Hutt.

"Dr. Robinson is still having financial problems due to his family. It's distracting him from his duties," Dr. Hutt said.

Ryder immediately felt defensive. "We need to look

for a solution instead of immediately booting him out of the program."

"I agree," Hutt said, surprising Ryder with his response.

"What about your princess friend?" he asked, leaning back in his chair. "Wouldn't this be a perfect solution? She gives him a bonus scholarship, he takes a tour of her country. Win, win."

"Are you serious?" Ryder asked.

"Yes," he said. "You and I must manage residents from all eco-social backgrounds. Not everyone is from your background. Not everyone is from mine."

For the first time in months, he felt a measure of hope. Maybe, just maybe Hutt could see past his privileged upbringing. "Are you sure you shouldn't push him harder?" he asked. "Maybe he just needs to work more."

His colleague frowned. "He's already working hard. Harder than I ever did," he said.

Ryder was stunned. He'd never known Hutt was capable of such insight. "When did this change happen?"

"The last time you and I met, I went home and couldn't sleep. For several nights. Dr. Walters not only kicked my butt, he also *encouraged* you. He wasn't one man to the residents. He stepped into their shoes and gave them what they needed. As advisers, we have to do the same."

Ryder shook his head. "When in hell did you become a reasonable man?"

His colleague laughed. "It's amazing the kind of perspective a wife can offer when you choose to talk to her."

"Your wife did this?" Ryder asked.

Hutt shrugged. "Professionally speaking, of course, she didn't," he said.

Ryder felt a change click through him and extended his hand to Dr. Hutt. "Give my best to your wife," he said.

"And give my best to your princess," Hutt said.

One day later, Bridget called him. He was in surgery, so he checked his messages. "Meet me today. Name the time," she said. "I have good news."

His day was crazy, but he managed to meet her at a quiet cocktail bar after work.

"Rough day?" she asked as she sipped a martini.

He felt a crazy surge of disappointment. The last couple of days, he'd secretly begun to like the idea of having a baby with Bridget. "You're not pregnant."

"I'm not," she said and lifted her glass to his. She smiled in relief. "Cheers."

"Cheers," he said. "And damn."

She blinked. "Damn?"

"Maybe I could have forced you into a shotgun marriage if you were pregnant."

She laughed and took another sip of her martini. "I wouldn't want a shotgun wedding for you or me," she said.

"I don't know," he said. "I think we could have made the best of it."

She sucked in a deep breath and glanced away. "Perhaps, but now we don't have to," she said with a shaky smile. She bit her lip. "My other news is that another medical center has stepped forward to participate in our program."

Surprised, Ryder searched her gaze. "Really?"

"We finally have doctors willing to come to Chantaine," she said, relief crossing her face. "I followed your advice and found experts willing to visit Chantaine and give training. And this medical center is willing to offer our scholarship and package to their residents. So far, two have signed up for our program. They weren't our first choice, but Stefan is confident this arrangement will be in the best interest of the country."

"Wow," Ryder said. "What a coincidence. Today Dr. Hutt and I agreed to send one of our residents to Chantaine. He's a talented generalist, but he has financial issues you can solve. Still interested?"

"Of course," she said. "I shouldn't say we're desperate, but we're definitely open. We're also going to need a new director for Chantaine's Health Center, but that's clearly a work in progress."

"I guess this means you're headed for Chantaine… or Italy," he said, his gut tightening into a square knot.

"Not right away, but very soon," she said. "I'll go back with Phillipa."

Chapter Twelve

Ryder returned home well after 9:00 p.m. after meeting Bridget for cocktails and dinner. He had arranged for Suzanne to stay late to watch the twins, but Marshall greeted him.

Marshall handed him a beer. "Hey, big guy. Congratulate me. Suzanne and I got married this weekend in Vegas. I sent her home because she was tired out. I kept her pretty busy this weekend," he added with a wink.

Stunned for the third time today, Ryder stared at Marshall. "What?"

"Suzanne and I got married. Don't worry, she's determined to still be your nanny even though I told her she could be a lady of leisure."

Ryder accepted the beer and took a sip. "Oh, Lord help me."

"That's not quite a congrats, but I'll take it," Marshall

said, giving Ryder a fist bump. "You look kinda strange, big guy. What's up?"

Ryder shook his head and sank onto his couch. "Just a crazy day. Are you sure Suzanne is still going to take care of the twins?"

Marshall sat on the other side of the couch. "Yeah. She's determined. You know she can't have babies, right? That's why her husband left her. His stupidity, my good luck."

"Bridget mentioned something about it," Ryder said, his mind falling back a few days to when her pregnancy had still been a possibility. And now she would be leaving soon. He knew the twins would miss her.

"Yeah, I told her there's more than one way to crack that nut. Getting a baby. We'll check out the IVF stuff, then we'll look into our adoption options. She was surprised I would be open to that. She's an amazing woman. I would do anything for her," Marshall said.

"Why didn't you tell me you were going to do this?" Ryder demanded.

"You'd already warned me away from Suzanne, but I wanted to get to know her. It took some work to get her to go out with me, but I knew she was the one for me. She's the first really good woman I've met and I knew I didn't want to let her go."

Ryder felt a twist of envy that Marshall had been able to overcome the obstacles that might have kept him and Suzanne apart. "Congratulations," he said, extending his hand.

Marshall nodded and smiled. "Still can't believe I was able to talk her into eloping. Of course, now is the hard part, but with her, I don't think it's gonna be that hard."

"She's a strong woman. If anyone can keep you in line, she's the one," Ryder said.

"Yeah, speaking of women, what's up with your princess?"

Ryder's gut tightened again. "I think she's headed back to Chantaine soon."

Marshall's eyebrows lifted in surprise. "Whoa. I thought you two—"

"Temporary," Ryder said. "For Pete's sake, she's a princess, and I've got my hands full with the boys and my position at the hospital."

"Hmm," Marshall said. "I could have sworn you two had it going on. Shame you couldn't work it out. Sorry, bud," he said and thumped Ryder on the shoulder. "Hope you don't mind, but my *wife* is waiting for me at home."

"Okay, okay," Ryder said with a faint smile. "Just make sure she gets enough sleep to take care of the boys."

Marshall just gave a dirty laugh and walked out the door.

Ryder stared into the distance and felt more alone than ever. For the most part, he hadn't minded being alone. In the past, it had meant he had to take care of only himself. All that had changed when his brother had died and Ryder had taken on the twins. Now it was just him and the twins.

An image of Bridget floated through his mind and he got an itchy, unsettled feeling inside him. Trying to dismiss it, he went to the kitchen and glanced through the mail for the day, but that itchy feeling didn't go away.

Ryder rubbed at his gut, but it didn't do any good. A sense of dread that started in his stomach climbed to the back of his throat.

Ryder swore under his breath. He'd fallen for the woman. Worse yet, he'd begun to rely on her. He, who relied on no one but himself. Shaking his head, he called himself ten kinds of fools. A princess? Putting his trust in anyone was dangerous, but a princess. Talk about impossible situations.

He ground his teeth. She was leaving. He needed to get used to the idea immediately. He needed to cut every thought of her from his mind.

Bridget felt ripped apart at the prospect of leaving Ryder and the boys, but she couldn't stall any longer. She'd completed her assignment and it was time for her to return to Chantaine before she took her long-delayed gap year in Italy. Somehow, she couldn't work up the same kind of excitement she'd felt during the last two years about finally taking a break.

She didn't know which upset her most: leaving Ryder and the twins or the fact that Ryder had ignored all of her calls. Desperate to make arrangements to see him one last time, she took matters into her own hands, went to the hospital and parked herself in his office when his assistant was away from her desk. She wasn't going through any gatekeepers this time.

After forty-five minutes of waiting, she saw Ryder finally open his office door. He looked at her and his expression registered shock, then all emotion seemed to vanish from his face. "Hello, Bridget. Sorry, I don't have time to visit."

His remoteness stabbed her. "I understand. I just didn't want to leave without seeing you and the twins again."

"Why? We won't be a part of your life anymore. There's no need to pretend we were anything more than a phase."

She dropped her jaw, surprised at his evaluation of the time they'd shared. "A phase?" she repeated in disbelief. "Is that all I was to you? A phase?"

Ryder gave a bitter laugh. "There's no need for drama. Both of us knew this was coming. It just came a little sooner than expected. I appreciate everything you did to help the twins. You provided a needed diversion for all three of us."

"A diversion," she said, feeling herself begin to shake.

"Don't get so upset. We knew from the beginning that there was no future to our relationship. I sure as hell am not the right man to be a princess's husband and you're not the type of woman to put up with a doctor's demanding schedule."

She felt as if he'd slapped her. He made her sound like she was a selfish, high-maintenance shrew. She bit the inside of her lip. "I had no idea you thought so little of me." She swallowed over the lump in her throat. "You really had me fooled. I've spent the last few days searching for ways to continue to see you and be with you. I realize it would be the ultimate long-distance relationship, but I couldn't bear the idea of not being in your life. I fell for both you and the boys." Her voice broke and she looked away, shaking her head. "At least, I fell for who I thought you were. I thought you felt the same way, but clearly I was—"

"No," he said, gripping her shoulders. She looked up and saw in his eyes that he was as tortured as she was. "No, you weren't wrong. I fell for you, too, much more than I intended. I've spent the last days telling myself to forget you. I know that's impossible, but I have to try."

Her eyes filled with tears. "I don't want you to forget me. I don't want you to speak about us in the past tense. You—you've become so important to me."

He winced as if in pain. "But it can't work. Our lives are just too different. We need to make it easy for each other to get used to the facts. The fact is you have to return to your country. You have responsibilities there. I have mine here."

She tried hard to hang on to her composure, but she couldn't. It hurt too much. She dropped her forehead against his chest. "This is so hard," she said, feeling tears streak down her face.

"It is," he said, sliding his hand through her hair and holding her close.

"Promise me you won't forget me," she said and lifted her gaze to look at him. "Give me that much."

"Never," he promised. "Never," he said and lowered his mouth to hers for a kiss. Their last kiss.

Ryder couldn't remember a time when he had felt like his guts had been ripped out and put through a grinder. Every waking moment, he was aware of the breathtaking pain. He tried, but couldn't block the sight of Bridget's tears from his mind. The way she'd felt in his arms. He would never feel that again. He would never feel that sense of unexpected joy just by seeing her smile or hearing her tease him.

Swearing under his breath as he arrived home, he ripped open the top few buttons of his shirt. Not only was he in mental hell, but the hot Dallas weather seemed to be determined to put him in physical hell, too.

"Hey, big guy," Marshall said as he held one of the twins while Suzanne changed the diaper of the other. "You don't look too good. Did you lose someone on the table today?"

One of the babies squealed at the sight of him. The sound gave Ryder a slight lift. He walked over and gave each baby a hug.

"No, I didn't lose a patient. Just got some things on my mind. Sorry I'm late. Tomorrow should be better."

He saw Marshall lift his eyebrows. "Hey, Suzy Q, how about I help you take the boys upstairs for a while. Ryder and I can drink a beer and watch a couple innings of a ball game. Are you okay with that?"

"Sure," she said. "I'll play some music and read to them."

Marshall gave his wife a firm kiss, then carried both boys upstairs.

A moment later, his friend returned. Ryder had already gotten two beers out of the fridge. "I don't want to talk about it," he muttered as he sank onto the couch.

"Okay," Marshall said and used the remote to turn on the TV. The Dallas team was losing again. Marshall swore. "They just can't pull it together."

"They need a different pitcher," Ryder said.

"They need a different everything," Marshall said.

Silence passed. "Suzanne tells me your princess stopped by today to give the boys some gifts before she returns to Champagne or wherever the hell she lives."

His gut twisted. Tomorrow. "It's Chantaine," he said.

"Whatever," Marshall said. "Suzanne said she held it together with the babies but fell apart on the front porch."

Ryder narrowed his eyes against another stab of emotion and took a quick breath. "It sucks all around."

"Hmm. Seems like a lot of unnecessary torture to me," Marshall said.

Ryder shot his friend a hard glance. "Unnecessary?" he asked.

"Well, yeah, if y'all are that miserable without each other, then stay together."

Impatience rippled through him. "Okay, Mr. Relationship Expert, exactly how would we do that?"

"Ask her to marry you. Ask her to stay," he said and took a sip of his beer. "Nice play," he said, nodding toward the screen.

Ignoring Marshall's comment on the game, Ryder set down his beer. "How in hell can I do that? She's a princess from another country and she works for her country. I work eighteen hours a day and I have twin boys. No woman in her right mind would agree to that kind of life. She deserves better."

"I take it to mean you didn't have the guts to ask her what she would want," he said.

Anger roared through him. "Guts? Who are you talking to about guts? Guts is what it takes to let her go."

"Hmm," Marshall said. "You know, Suzanne and I are gonna have a baby."

"She's pregnant already?" Ryder asked.

"No. We don't know *how* we're going to have a baby. We just know we will. I told you about this the other day, but you probably weren't listening. There are lots of ways to have a baby these days. IVF, surrogacy, adoption in the States, overseas..." He nodded. "Yep, they're putting in the second-string pitcher. Let's see what happens now."

"What's your point?" Ryder demanded.

"There's more than one way to crack a nut," he said. "There's more than one solution to a problem. You could ask Bridget to move here. You could commute for a while. Just because you commute for a while doesn't mean you'll have to do it forever. Hell, didn't you say her country needed some doctors? If you really wanted to, you could move to Champagne and be a doctor there."

"Chantaine," Ryder corrected, mentally dismissing Marshall's suggestions in one fell swoop.

"Well, my man, you're going to have to make some career changes anyway," Marshall said. "Those babies are little now, but when they get older they're going to need to have their daddy around more than an hour or two every day. You're gonna have to figure out what kind of father you want to be, and I'm guessing it's nothing like the father you had."

Ryder mused over that for a long moment. He'd been fighting change ever since his brother had died. Although he'd done his best with the twins, he'd clung to what was most familiar to him, and that was his career. Outside of the hospital, he'd felt completely out of control. For a time, Bridget had made the new responsibility he'd faced feel a little lighter. She'd even made it fun.

He wondered how she would have responded if he'd asked her to stay. If he'd asked her to marry him. His heart hammered at the ridiculous possibility. The very idea of it was ludicrous. Even more ridiculous was the idea of his quitting his position, uprooting the twins and moving across the world for a completely different life with the woman who had made him fall in love with her. She hadn't asked for that because she hadn't wanted it. Ryder scowled at Marshall. The man was just stirring up a bunch of craziness because he'd found and married the woman of his dreams.

"At least, we can be miserable together," Bridget said to Phillipa, adjusting her dark, oversized sunglasses as she and her sister strode through the airport. She planned on keeping these sunglasses on her face night and day, inside and outside except when she was in her private quarters. No amount of cosmetics concealed the gutted agony in her eyes.

"It would have been nice to have the private jet," Phillipa said.

"So true, but Stefan always gets first rights to the jet. Plus, it's supposed to be much less expensive to travel commercial on the long-haul flights. At least we'll be together in first class. Hopefully they'll have a distracting movie. Although with my luck, it will be one of those dreadful tales with an unhappy ending from that American author. What's his name?"

"Robert James Waller," Phillipa said. "I've never liked sad movies. I know that some people say crying is cleansing, but I hate it."

"Me, too," Bridget said.

"I don't mean to upset you, but did you ever even ask Dr. McCall if he wanted you to stay?"

Bridget's stomach twisted. "He said our future was

impossible. He didn't even want to discuss the possibility of our seeing each other after this trip back to Chantaine." She felt her throat tighten with emotion and took a tiny breath. "No hope," she said.

Pippa reached over to take her hand. "I'm so sorry. You seemed so different once you met him. I'd thought he might be the one."

Her heart stretching and tightening, Bridget squeezed her sister's hand. "I'm lucky to have such a sweet sister."

"Your Highness," Raoul said, stepping to Bridget's side. "I apologize for the interruption, but Dr. McCall has arrived at the airport. He wishes to speak to you. I must warn you that you don't have much ti—"

Shocked, thrilled, afraid to hope, she felt her breath lodge somewhere between her lungs and throat. "I will speak to him," she managed in a whisper that sounded hoarse to her own ears.

Seconds that felt like eons later, Ryder stood in front of her.

"Hi," he said, meeting her gaze dead-on.

Her heart was hammering so fast that she could hardly breathe. "Hi. What brings you here?"

He took a deep breath and cocked his head to one side. "You mentioned that your country needs a new medical director. I wondered if you thought I could handle the job?"

Stunned and confused, she shook her head. "Excuse me? Are you asking for the position?"

He paused a half beat, then nodded. "Yeah, I guess I am."

Torn between throwing herself in his arms and trying to keep her head from spinning, she bit her lip. "Would you like me to talk to Stefan? I'm sure he would be thrilled."

"That's good. How would you feel about it?" he asked. "How would you feel about the twins and me coming to Chantaine?"

Bridget was so light-headed that she feared she might faint. She grabbed the back of a chair. "I would be beyond thrilled."

"Thrilled enough to marry me?"

She gasped, unable to register his question. "Excuse me?"

He moved toward her and took her hands in his. "I love you. I want my future with you. I want my children's future with you. I know it's fast, but will you—"

"Yes," she said, her eyes filling with tears of joy. Her heart was overflowing. "Yes, yes and yes."

Ryder took her into his arms and she hugged him tightly. The secret dream of having a man love her just for herself had just come true.

Five months later, Bridget stood in front of Ryder in the chapel of the oldest church in Chantaine and pinched herself. Her sisters dabbed at tears with handkerchiefs. Her brother Stefan beamed his approval. He was so thrilled one of his siblings had finally made a marriage that would benefit Chantaine. With Ryder as the newly appointed medical director of Chantaine, there was no shortage of residents clamoring to come to their country. Her sister-in-law Eve gave her an encouraging nod. The twins ran along the side aisle like the wild rascals they were. Her youngest brother and Raoul chased after them. Bridget had reached a new level of terror when the boys had started pulling up, and worse, walking. Not one day passed, however, when she didn't thank God for Ryder and the boys.

The priest led them in their vows. Ryder's voice was clear and strong. His gaze was resolute. She knew she could count on this man for the rest of her life. Surprisingly enough, she knew he could count on her, too. Ryder's love had triggered something hidden deep inside her, something she'd hoped she possessed, but it had never surfaced. With Ryder in her life, she didn't mind her royal duties, yet she could say no to Stefan when necessary.

Even with all the sacrifices and changes Ryder had made, he seemed happier and more relaxed. At the same time, he saw many opportunities for improvement and expansion in Chantaine's health program. She still couldn't believe how everything had worked out. Every day, she grew closer to Ryder and fell more deeply in love with him. She counted her blessings that she would spend the rest of her life with him and the twins. Despite her best efforts, though, he refused to reveal his honeymoon plans. As long as it didn't involve the desert, and it did involve just the two of them, she would be happy.

With the twins squealing in delight, the priest appeared to smother a chuckle. "I now pronounce you husband and wife. You may kiss your bride," he said.

Ryder took her face in his hands as if it were the most precious thing in the world and lowered his mouth to hers. She threw her hands around his neck and kissed him with all her heart.

Distantly, she heard the sound of laughter and

applause. She pulled back and turned to the many witnesses seated in the chapel, glancing toward the twins.

Ryder's mind must have been moving in the same direction. "Tyler," he called. "Travis. Come here right now."

The twins turned suddenly solemn, but made their way to the front of the church. Dressed in pale blue short suits, both boys lifted their arms toward her and Ryder. Heedless of her designer wedding dress, she scooped up Tyler while Ryder picked up Travis.

"Ladies and gentlemen, may God bless this happy union."

As the group in the church applauded again, Ryder leaned toward her and kissed her again. "I'm taking you to Italy, Your Highness. Tomorrow."

* * * * *

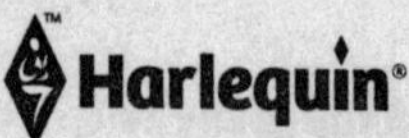

SPECIAL EDITION®

COMING NEXT MONTH

Available July 26, 2011

#2131 THE BABY WORE A BADGE
Marie Ferrarella
Montana Mavericks: The Texans are Coming!

#2132 COURTNEY'S BABY PLAN
Allison Leigh
Return to the Double C

#2133 BIG SKY BRIDE, BE MINE!
Victoria Pade
Northbridge Nuptials

#2134 THE MOMMY MIRACLE
Lilian Darcy

#2135 THE MOGUL'S MAYBE MARRIAGE
Mindy Klasky

#2136 LIAM'S PERFECT WOMAN
Beth Kery
Home to Harbor Town

HSECNM0711

Once bitten, twice shy. That's Gabby Wade's motto—
especially when it comes to Adamson men.
And the moment she meets Jon Adamson her theory
is confirmed. But with each encounter a little something
sparks between them, making her wonder if she's been
too hasty to dismiss this one!

Enjoy this sneak peek from ONE GOOD REASON
by Sarah Mayberry, available August 2011
from Harlequin® Superromance®.

Gabby Wade's heartbeat thumped in her ears as she marched to her office. She wanted to pretend it was because of her brisk pace returning from the file room, but she wasn't that good a liar.

Her heart was beating like a tom-tom because Jon Adamson had touched her. In a very male, very possessive way. She could still feel the heat of his big hand burning through the seat of her khakis as he'd steadied her on the ladder.

It had taken every ounce of self-control to tell him to unhand her. What she'd really wanted was to grab him by his shirt and, well, explore all those urges his touch had instantly brought to life.

While she might not like him, she was wise enough to understand that it wasn't always about liking the other person. Sometimes it was about pure animal attraction.

Refusing to think about it, she turned to work. When she'd typed in the wrong figures three times, Gabby admitted she was too tired and too distracted. Time to call it a day.

As she was leaving, she spied Jon at his workbench in the shop. His head was propped on his hand as he studied blueprints. It wasn't until she got closer that she saw his

HSREXP0811I

eyes were shut.

He looked oddly boyish. There was something innocent and unguarded in his expression. She felt a weakening in her resistance to him.

"Jon." She put her hand on his shoulder, intending to shake him awake. Instead, it rested there like a caress.

His eyes snapped open.

"You were asleep."

"No, I was, uh, visualizing something on this design." He gestured to the blueprint in front of him then rubbed his eyes.

That gesture dealt a bigger blow to her resistance. She realized it wasn't only animal attraction pulling them together. She took a step backward as if to get away from the knowledge.

She cleared her throat. "I'm heading off now."

He gave her a smile, and she could see his exhaustion.

"Yeah, I should, too." He stood and stretched. The hem of his T-shirt rose as he arched his back and she caught a flash of hard male belly. She looked away, but it was too late. Her mind had committed the image to permanent memory.

And suddenly she knew, for good or bad, she'd never look at Jon the same way again.

Find out what happens next in ONE GOOD REASON, available August 2011 from Harlequin® Superromance®!

HSREXP0811